SUMMER'S END
A COZY QUILTS CLUB MYSTERY
BOOK THREE

MARSHA DEFILIPPO

CONTENTS

Prologue	1
Chapter 1	5
Chapter 2	9
Chapter 3	11
Chapter 4	14
Chapter 5	17
Chapter 6	21
Chapter 7	24
Chapter 8	28
Chapter 9	33
Chapter 10	36
Chapter 11	42
Chapter 12	49
Chapter 13	53
Chapter 14	57
Chapter 15	63
Chapter 16	67
Chapter 17	74
Chapter 18	78
Chapter 19	82
Chapter 20	84
Chapter 21	89
Chapter 22	96
Chapter 23	98
Chapter 24	100
Chapter 25	104
Chapter 26	107
Chapter 27	109
Chapter 28	112
Chapter 29	118
Chapter 30	120
Chapter 31	123
Chapter 32	127
Chapter 33	130

Chapter 34	136
Chapter 35	140
Chapter 36	143
Chapter 37	147
Chapter 38	149
Chapter 39	152
Chapter 40	154
Chapter 41	156
Epilogue	159
Afterword	161
Also by Marsha DeFilippo	163
About the Author	165

Copyright © 2023 by Marsha DeFilippo

All rights reserved.

This is a work of fiction. Unless otherwise indicated, all the names, characters, businesses, places, events and incidents in this book are either the product of the author's imagination or used in a fictitious manner. Any resemblance to actual persons, living or dead, or actual events is purely coincidental.

No part of this book may be reproduced in any form or by any electronic or mechanical means, including information storage and retrieval systems, without written permission from the author, except for the use of brief quotations in a book review.

For avoidance of doubt, Marsha DeFilippo reserves the rights, and publishers/platforms have no rights to, reproduce and/or otherwise use the Work in any manner for purposes of training artificial intelligence technologies to generate text, including without limitation, technologies that are capable of generating works in the same style or genre as the Work, unless publisher/platform obtains Marsha DeFilippo's specific and express permission to do so. Nor does publishers/platforms have the right to sublicense others to reproduce and/or otherwise use the Work in any manner for purposes of training artificial intelligence technologies to generate text without Marsha DeFilippo's specific and express permission.

To get the latest information on new releases, excerpts and more, be sure to sign up for Marsha's newsletter.

https://marshadefilippo.com/newsletter

PROLOGUE

"I really should have done this earlier," Summer Williams said out loud although no one else was with her. She was only a mile from her house, but already sweating, and her tee shirt was starting to cling to her back. She looked up at the brilliant azure blue sky hoping to see clouds but there was not a one in sight to deflect the intensity of the sunshine. The day started out comfortably, but the temperature and humidity on this late August mid-afternoon had climbed by the time she decided to take a run. The baseball cap she had put on to stop the sun from beating on her head helped to shade her eyes and face but even it wasn't enough. She wiped away a bead of sweat trickling its way downward from her forehead toward her temple to keep it from running into her eyes.

Summer was heading into her senior year of high school and had been on the school's track team for the past three years. It wasn't a guarantee she would automatically be selected for a varsity spot again; she'd still have to try out, so taking a day off from her training was not negotiable. Being on JV wouldn't be the end of the world, but making varsity was goal number one. What she really wanted to accomplish, though, was competing in the Boston Marathon the following April. It would be her first time and she needed to be prepared physically and mentally.

The only sounds were the pounding of her footsteps on the pavement of the rural road, the occasional squawks of crows overhead, and crickets in the grass beside the shoulder. Her blonde ponytail that she had threaded through the gap in the back of her baseball cap swung back and forth with the rhythm of her steps. She had thought about wearing her AirPods to listen to music while she ran to keep her distracted from the fatigue which hit about an hour into the run, but her mother had been on her case again. It was her preference that Summer use the treadmill in their basement, but compromised by insisting she not wear the AirPods so she would be focused on any approaching cars. Though the houses on this part of Glen Lake were more spaced-out than other areas, the road which cut through this section was a secondary route to several nearby towns, which meant it still had a lot of traffic. In some sections sharp curves prevented a driver from seeing what might be around the corners and they were more likely to be looking for oncoming vehicles than pedestrians. As Summer neared one of those, she thought she could hear a car, but it sounded like it was still in the distance. She calculated how long it would take, and decided she would have no trouble making it to the curve and getting past it before the vehicle reached her. As she rounded the corner, she tried to make sense of what she was seeing. The car had gotten closer faster than she'd anticipated which surprised her, but the bigger shock was that it had no driver. Her brain was still processing this as she moved over to the shoulder of the road, wary now and unsure of what to do, but thinking she might have to jump into the grassy area beyond the breakdown lane even though it sloped down into a gully. Although it had been going straight, it was now drifting off the pavement and onto the gravel heading directly toward her. She'd waited too long. The car's front fender clipped her right side, and she was thrown into the air, landing in the gully, hidden by the overgrown grass.

LUNCH AT NANCY'S had been exactly what she needed to get out of her end of summer slump. She hadn't laughed that much in months. The food was mouth-watering delicious and the wine! Had she had two glasses or three? None is what she should have had, but the DUI on her record happened five years ago. Surely it wasn't something to worry about now. She was driving just fine and only felt a little buzzed. No need to be concerned.

She was going a little faster than the speed limit, but the traffic was light today. She hadn't seen another vehicle on the road for miles. The radio's volume was loud, and she was bouncing with the beat, doing her best car dance to match her mood. It was a hot day, and the air conditioning was on full blast; another reason for having the music turned up. She jumped when her phone rang, and she realized she'd forgotten to plug it in to enable the hands-free feature. It was still in her pocketbook on the passenger seat. Even though she knew she shouldn't, she glanced away from the road to try to pull it out to see who was calling and it slipped onto the floorboard. She looked back up to confirm she was still going straight, and no cars were coming, then bent over to pick up her purse to put it back on the seat. She would have to be quick about it as she was getting close to the curve up ahead and eased up on the gas pedal to give herself more time. When she felt the impact and a loud thud sounded from the passenger side, she reflexively yanked the steering wheel to the left and popped back up to find she had drifted toward the shoulder. Once fully back on the pavement she jammed on the brakes, her tires screeching. Her eyes flew to the rearview mirror, but all she saw was the highway stretching out behind her. Confused, she was certain she hadn't imagined it but if she did hit something, where was it?

It must have been an animal that came out of the bushes and then ran back. If I killed it, it would be lying on the road, she rationalized. She'd heard accounts of that happening many times over the years, especially when it involved a deer. *Even if I went back, what could I do about it if it was still there?* The argument worked and though her cheerful mood was now history, and her conscience wasn't completely buying it, she continued on her way home, her complete attention on her driving. Her purse would have to stay where it was until then and if whoever had been calling tried again, they would just have to leave a voice mail.

CHAPTER ONE

*K*aren LeBlanc was finishing up weeding the flower beds in her front yard; a chore she'd put off the past two days. It had only taken half an hour, but she was starting to stiffen up. *I used to be able to do this all day ten years ago;* she thought, missing those times. She stood up, placed her hands on her hips and arched back slightly feeling a satisfying pop in her lower spine. It had been quiet for most of the time she'd been outside, so the car heading toward Bangor caught her attention. It was approaching the curve in the road at the same time as a young woman came running around the corner. The runner's identity suddenly registered, and she watched in horror as the car drifted onto the shoulder toward her.

Get out of the way, Summer! she shouted. Even after she had time to think about it later, she wasn't sure if she actually said that out loud or it had all been in her head. It happened so quickly the logical side of her brain knew it wouldn't have made a difference, but there was the emotional side that still wondered if she could have done more.

The impact of the car hitting her body threw Summer into the air and into the tall grass where the edge of the road sloped down into the gully below. Karen was momentarily paralyzed but then, her hands shaking, pulled her cell phone from her pocket intending to dial 911. The car came to a screeching stop, and she expected the driver to get out to help, but instead, after remaining motionless for a minute, it continued on its way. It was too far away to read the license plate number and she'd never been one to recognize the make of vehicles, but she could tell it was a silver, four-door sedan. She dialed 911 and began to run toward the spot where she'd seen Summer land in the grass. The dispatcher came on the line, but Karen kept running.

"911. What is your emergency?"

"There's been an accident on the Hudson Road in Glen Lake. A car hit Summer Williams and then drove away. I'm going down now to see how badly she's hurt. You'll need to send an ambulance... NOW!"

"What is your location?"

Karen gave the dispatcher her house address and added that the scene of the accident was about three hundred feet past it heading toward Bangor.

"After I've checked on Summer, I'll keep a watch for the ambulance and flag it down if I can."

"I'll stay on the line until you've found her. Did you get a description of the vehicle?"

"I couldn't see the license plate number, but it's a silver four-door sedan."

"Were you able to see the driver?"

"Not really, but I think it was a woman. The car was too far away from me to tell for sure. I'm sorry it all happened so fast, and they drove away before I could get a good look," she said, her frustration coming through. *I had my phone in my hand. Why didn't I take a picture of the car?*

"That's okay, ma'am. Have you found the victim?"

"Summer. Her name is Summer. And no, I'm still on my way."

Karen was panting from exertion by the time she reached the spot where she thought the car had stopped. *I have got to start exercising more.* The thought darted into her head, and she chastised herself about how trivial that was compared to the importance of why she was here and then flitted back out as she focused on her mission.

Fresh tire skid marks were on the road up ahead, so Karen knew she had to be in the right location, but Summer was nowhere to be seen. She carefully made her way down the slope to the spot where she thought her body must have landed, calling out Summer's name. No answer came, and she prayed it was because Summer was unconscious. Karen realized as soon as she found her body lying still in the grass, her prayer was not going to be answered. She put her fingers on Summer's wrist to check for a pulse but there was none.

"I've found her," she said, her voice almost a whisper. "She's dead."

"Are you sure?"

"I can't feel a pulse and she isn't breathing."

Karen looked up as the sound of a siren approaching caught her attention.

"I think the ambulance is coming now, so I'm going to go back up to the road to wave them down."

"I'll stay on the line with you until they arrive."

"Thank you," was all she could manage as she fought to maintain her composure and wiped away the tears that ran down her cheeks.

She spotted the vehicle, but it was a sheriff's car, not the ambulance. Standing on the shoulder, she waved her arms in the air and it slowed down, pulling off the road a few yards in front of her. The officer got out of the car and jogged over to her.

"An officer is here now so I'm going to disconnect."

"Alright, ma'am," the dispatcher replied, and the call ended.

"I'm Deputy Tremblay, ma'am. I got a call about a hit and run accident."

"Yes, I'm the one who called. You can't see her from here. She's down in the grass," Karen said looking over to where she'd found Summer, "but it's too late. Follow me and I'll show you."

They scrambled down the slope to the spot where Summer was lying, and Deputy Tremblay repeated what Karen had already done. His head remained bowed for several seconds before he rose to his feet and turned to Karen.

"Do you know who she is?"

"Her name is Summer Williams. She's in the same class as my daughter. She lives here on the Hudson Road about a mile beyond the curve in the road, but I'm not sure of the number. It's on this side and is a blue raised ranch. Oh my god, how will Debbie and Roger survive this?" The question was rhetorical but voicing it aloud broke the dam of emotions she'd held in until now and the sobs racked her body.

CHAPTER TWO

∼

*O*nce she returned home, she parked her car in the garage and checked for damage. The passenger side headlight was broken and there was a dent in the front fender, but it could have been worse. One of her friend's cars was totaled after hitting a deer, so all things considered, it wasn't terrible. Tomorrow would be soon enough to call the repair shop to have it fixed. The aftereffects of the adrenaline rush and the wine she'd imbibed with lunch took hold along with the heat of the day now that she was safely back at home, and the only thing she wanted to do was go inside and take a nap.

She woke up two hours later, but the nap had left her groggy and her head felt as though it was stuffed with cotton. *Maybe a cup of coffee might help.* She shuffled over to the coffeemaker intending to set it up for a single serving but stopped, worried the caffeine would keep her up. Instead, she poured a glass of water and drank it down. By then it was dinner time, but she had no desire to cook and the last thing she wanted to do was get back in her car, even for a run for fast food. Giving silent thanks that she kept a supply of frozen dinners in the freezer for occasions such as this, she picked out the single serving pepperoni pizza. The microwave dinged bringing her out of her stupor and she took it to the living room to eat while she watched the evening news.

The lead story was about a hit and run accident in Glen Lake earlier in the day. Her focus had been more on her meal than the television, but the mention of Glen Lake caught her attention and she hit the rewind button on the remote. The anchor reporting the story was saying a witness identified the vehicle as a silver four-door sedan which stopped briefly but then left the scene after the accident. Eighteen-year-old Summer Williams was declared dead at the scene. She had been training for her high school track team and was planning to run in the Boston Marathon for the first time next year...

She sat transfixed in horror but the sound of the words coming from the television were muffled in her ears as the realization washed over her that she had to be the driver who had fled from the scene. The timing and location of the accident matched what had happened and she drove a silver four-door sedan. It hadn't been an animal at all. She catapulted from her seat, the plate in her lap tumbling to the floor. Putting her hand over her mouth, she ran to the bathroom, her stomach ejecting its contents into the toilet.

CHAPTER THREE

Jennifer Ryder mentally checked off the list of things she needed to take with her as she prepared to go to her weekly quilt club meeting. She and three other women formed the club a few months prior after being introduced while at a class at their local quilt store. The women bonded first over their hobby and then worked as a team to solve two murders and elicit a confession from the killers. The first case hit close to home as one of the two victims had been Jennifer's great-aunt, Sadie Emerson, who lived across the street from her house. Being an amateur sleuth would have been unusual on its own in their little bedroom community, but more unusual was how they discovered the identities of the killers. Each of the four women had their own paranormal skill. Jennifer's was psychometry and the image she'd received while wearing a ring she inherited from her aunt played an instrumental part. Her fellow quilt club member, Eva Perkins, possessed a unique ability to communicate with animals. This skill enabled her to gain valuable information from Boscoe,

Sadie's Jack Russell terrier. It was Boscoe who revealed the murderer's name; without his help, the truth of what happened on that fateful night might never have been discovered. When they told the killer details about what he'd done and how he was dressed on the night of the murder, it shocked him into defending his actions and without his being aware of it, they recorded his confession on their phones. A month later, fellow member Annalise Jordan's house had been broken into and her psychic visions combined with the fourth member, Sarah Pascal's, ability to communicate with ghosts had given them the information they needed to discover the identity of the would-be burglars and solve a related murder.

"I shouldn't be any later than usual, hon, but if you need me, you know how to find me," she said giving her husband a peck on the cheek. David Ryder looked up from his task of chopping vegetables for the tossed salad he was making to go with the spaghetti already boiling on the stove.

"Take as long as you need. I think we can take care of ourselves for a few hours," he said, giving her a wink.

Boscoe jumped up from his bed, trotted over to Jennifer, and barked to let her know he wanted a goodbye pat. He came to live with the Ryders after Sadie's death and soon became one of the family. Jennifer bent down to scratch under his chin and behind his ears as he turned his head to help her reach the sweet spots.

"You be a good boy. I'll be back soon."

Woof!

Boscoe trotted back to his bed, circled two times to find just the right spot, and then laid down with his front paws under his chin.

She picked up her purse and dish for the potluck supper and was about to leave when her son, Matthew, suddenly sat upright in his chair at the kitchen table. He was holding his cell phone, reading a text, the contents of which she could see by his expression had to be bad news.

"What's wrong, Matt?"

"Summer Williams is dead. She was killed this afternoon by a hit and run driver while she was out running on the Hudson Road." He looked up at Jennifer in disbelief and shock.

Before she had time to reply, her daughter, Nicole, received a text message as well.

"Oh, no, it must be true. Ellie texted me the same news," she said, tears welling up in her eyes.

"Are they sure?"

Both teenagers had been texting back to whomever was on the other end.

"Andy Nichols said Christine LeBlanc told him about it. Her mom saw it happen when she was outside working in her yard and called 911 but Summer was already dead."

"That's what Ellie said, too," Nicole said.

"Are you alright? Should I stay home?" Jennifer asked, putting her purse back.

"I'll be okay, Mom. Go to your meeting," Matthew said.

"Me, too. And Dad's here," Nicole agreed.

Jennifer looked at David for his reaction.

"We'll be okay. We can talk when you get home. Maybe we'll have more details by then."

Jennifer nodded and gave Matthew and Nicole a hug, wanting the reassurance of physical touch more for herself than them and gave a silent prayer of thanks that her children were safe and sound.

"If you change your minds, I'm only a phone call away."

CHAPTER FOUR

∼

*A*s she drove to the meeting, Jennifer reflected on how an event like this affected the entire community. In a town like Glen Lake which only had five thousand residents, many of whose families had lived there for generations, connections by six degrees of separation were an established fact, not merely a theory. There would be few who wouldn't have some relationship to Summer or her family even if it was only on the periphery and the news of her death would quickly spread.

As Jennifer passed by houses along the way to Eva Perkins's house, she was able in most cases to identify its occupants by name. She had lived in Glen Lake all her life, as had David, and the town hadn't changed much. True, it had more subdivisions, a *lot* more subdivisions, than when she was a little girl, but it still had very few businesses. The notable ones were two convenience stores on opposite sides of the town and only one restaurant, a diner which was attached to one of the convenience stores. Five years ago, a Family Dollar store had been the buzz of the town when they opened a location on the Hudson Road which was one of only two major streets, roads would be more accurate, which ran through the town. Unlike nearby Bangor which was laid out in the usual grids of streets and cross streets found in cities, in Glen Lake the majority were within the various subdivisions that branched off the main roads. The town's one school was an elementary level with grades kindergarten through eighth grade and once they'd graduated, students attended their choice of the nearby communities' high schools. Despite the lack of stores to shop in or eating establishments, most residents felt they had the best of both worlds since whenever they wanted the conveniences it provided, Bangor was only ten miles away from Glen Lake's farthest borders.

Unless Summer's parents decided her memorial would be private, Jennifer knew the town would rally together to make sure her passing would be a celebration of her life and it would be standing room only. Summer's outgoing personality and cheerful disposition endeared her to everyone. She had made her mark on the town in her brief lifetime and her popularity extended beyond her peers. Once she was old enough, she became involved in community projects including volunteering for the town's Recreation Department's summer programs, the town's annual Glen Lake Days celebration which took place every July, and various events put on by the elementary school.

Jennifer's thoughts shifted to Summer's parents. The pain they must be feeling to have their child taken away from them so suddenly and senselessly was beyond comprehension. Tears began to fill her eyes and she had to take a deep breath and blink to stay focused on the road. Going down that path thinking about what it would have been like if it had been Matthew or Nicole would open the floodgates. That the driver had left the scene was the final insult. She hoped the person responsible would either come to their senses and confess to the crime regardless of the consequences, or enough evidence would be uncovered for the police to locate and arrest them.

Her musings ended when she reached Eva Perkins's house and turned into the driveway for the quilt club meeting. Usually, she looked forward to the meetings as the highlight of her week. As well as providing a creative outlet, it gave her a break from the daily routine of working part-time with David at their insurance agency and mom duties. Tonight, though, her heart wasn't in it, and she almost wished she'd called to say she wouldn't be coming. The other part of her understood, though, that she needed the support of the ladies in the club. They had not been friends very long, but the bond they had formed was strong.

CHAPTER FIVE

"Jennifer, what's wrong?" Eva Perkins said as soon as she opened the door to let her in. Jennifer's expression left no doubt she was in emotional distress. "Let me help you with that," she offered, taking the covered dish from Jennifer and putting one arm around her shoulders. "Just leave the rest of your stuff for now and come out to the kitchen. The others are already here, and you can tell all of us what has you upset."

Jennifer allowed herself to be led into the kitchen where Annalise Jordan and Sarah Pascal were seated at the center island. Their faces mirrored Eva's concern upon seeing Jennifer.

"What's happened?" Annalise asked.

The three sat quietly, their faces registering shock and dismay, as Jennifer told them of Summer's death and that the driver had left the scene before first responders arrived.

"I don't have many details other than that Karen LeBlanc was working in her yard when it happened and she's the one who called 911."

"I've met Summer's mother, Debbie, a few times at community events, but I don't know her well," Annalise said. "Whenever I saw her and Summer together, I could tell they were close. This is going to hit hard."

"This is so horrible! Have they caught up with the driver yet?" Sarah asked.

"I don't think so, but the kids got the news just as I was about to come here."

"I'm so sorry, Jen. Did Matthew or Nicole know Summer well?" Eva asked.

"They were together all through elementary school here in Glen Lake and my kids chose to go to the same high school as she went to. She is... was... in her senior year, the same as Matt. He's been in some of her classes, and they studied together on occasion. Nicole is two years behind so they didn't have any classes together, but she was on the track team with Summer once she got to high school. Summer has been on the varsity team and was training to run in the Boston Marathon next April. She was probably out for a run as part of her training for that."

"I can't imagine what her parents must be going through. They must be devastated," Eva said.

"She was a terrific kid. Honor student. The kids said she planned to go to UMaine next year and wanted to earn her degree as an elementary school teacher. She loved kids and was in high demand for babysitting."

They were interrupted by the doorbell and when Eva passed through the living room on her way to the front door, her Maine coon cat, Reuben, announced it was Sharon Ramos and Paul Taylor was right behind her. They didn't attend the meetings on a regular basis but were welcome additions to the club when they were able to come. By using her abilities as an animal whisperer, Eva and Reuben were able to communicate.

"Thanks, Reuben!"

I live to serve, he drawled from his cushion, or throne, as he thought of it.

Eva opened the door to let them in. Sharon was Annalise Jordan's cousin and was joining the other ladies at the meetings while she was in Maine. Later in the autumn she would be returning to Arizona with her husband, Joseph, where they lived the other half of the year. Paul Taylor was an employee at Quilting Essentials, the shop where the group had first met and was also a quilter.

"We're all gathered in the kitchen. Jennifer was telling us some sad news she found out before coming to the meeting. One of her kids' classmates was killed by a hit and run driver this afternoon."

"Oh, that's awful," Sharon said.

When they got to the kitchen, Jennifer gave Sharon and Paul an account of the news she'd told the others. They were all silent after she finished.

"I've got an idea," Eva said, breaking the silence. "We were going to pick a new project tonight. I'd like to propose that we all make a quilt to donate to Project Linus in Summer's memory."

"Project Linus?" Sarah asked, her brow furrowed.

"It's an organization which takes donations of blankets to give out to children. They can be knit, crochet, or quilts. The primary requirement is that they be homemade."

"That's a fabulous idea!" Jennifer agreed.

"We're a drop off location for blankets at the quilt shop. Just bring them in once you're done," Paul offered.

"Thank you, Paul. I didn't realize you were one of the drop off places but having one so close will make it much easier," Eva said.

"What if we each make a quilt that has summer as part of the name of the design?" Annalise suggested.

The others enthusiastically agreed. The somber mood lifted as excitement about the project replaced it.

"I can bring out my quilt books for us to look through. If we can't find anything in those, we can always check the internet," Eva offered and received nods of approval. "Now that we have that part of our agenda settled, how about we have our dinner?"

CHAPTER SIX

∼

The next morning, she got up early. It had been a waste of time even trying to sleep, as all she'd accomplished was tossing and turning thinking about what she'd done.

She had convinced herself she couldn't go to the police. Leaving the scene of the accident was a serious offense even though she hadn't realized it was a person she'd hit, and she didn't have anyone with her to back her up. *If there had been, they could have picked up my phone and it never would have happened in the first place,* she thought, but heard the petulance of the voice in her head. *You just killed a young girl and you're thinking about how unfair it is for* you? the other voice admonished, and she decided to drop that line of conversation.

Combine leaving the scene with her previous DUI on her record and the best she could hope for would be a conviction on the charge of manslaughter. That is, *if* she was able to convince them the only reason she left is because she didn't see anything in the road when she stopped and assumed it had been a deer. It would mean the ruin of her reputation and who would hire her after serving time in jail? She was nowhere near retirement age, and she would probably lose her house. She had money in her savings account but would it last if she was in jail for... *how long? Years? And who would take care of the house in the meantime? Not to mention having to hire an attorney to defend me.*

She didn't have answers for those questions despite having had them running through her head all night long. She had to do something about the damage to her car, though, and soon. They were already looking for a silver four-door sedan and with the damage to her headlight and bumper she might as well just put a sign on it saying **It was me**. She couldn't keep driving it around town in that condition.

But she couldn't go to her car dealership either. She'd watched enough crime shows to know they were probably being asked to notify the police if anyone showed up with a car like hers to have repairs made. She would have to find someplace outside of Bangor, and it might be best to find a small independent repair shop that wouldn't be as likely to be on their radar. And she would have to pay cash so there wouldn't be any charges showing up on her credit cards. She might be able to spare five thousand dollars, but *it wouldn't cost that much, would it?* Yet another question she had no answer for, but the first bridge to cross was finding a repair shop. Having at least the seed of a plan, she opened her laptop and typed in auto repair shops using the incognito option that claimed to hide her browser history from being visible on her computer. *That is what that means, isn't it?* She shrugged her shoulders in response and decided it didn't matter. *No point getting hung up on that when she had more important things to figure out.* If her car was fixed, who would know? There hadn't been any other cars on the road when she'd stopped, so no witnesses. The police couldn't possibly investigate every person who owned a silver four-door sedan. *Just get the car fixed and no one will be the wiser. And act normal!*

She took a deep breath and resolved to follow that advice.

CHAPTER SEVEN

Matthew and Nicole arrived home from their first day of school two days later and Jennifer noticed they were much more subdued than usual.

"How was your first day?"

"They have grief counselors for anyone who needs to talk about Summer," Nicole told her.

"There's already talk around school it was Lacey Daniels who ran her down. She's on the track team, too, and has always been jealous of Summer. She made some trouble for her at the beginning of last year, but it never got far because everyone knows Summer wasn't a cheater like Lacey claimed," Matthew said.

"Plus, everyone knows Lacey is part of the mean girls clique. What's that saying, consider the source? I think that's what I've heard you say, Mom," Nicole said looking to her mother for confirmation.

"It's not quite what that means, but I get the gist," Jennifer said.

"Did either of you speak with a grief counselor?" Jennifer kept her tone casual. She'd been watching them since they'd heard the news of Summer's death. After the initial shock she hadn't spotted any signs that their behavior changed. They'd both been busy getting ready for the start of the new school year and had practices for their track and soccer teams even before school began. That helped take the focus off the tragedy, but she worried they could be holding in their feelings.

Matt was the first to answer.

"I went to the group session with my class. We told stories about things we'd done with Summer. Most of them were funny because that's what we remember about her. She was a lot of fun and always had a smile on her face. If anyone wanted to have a private meeting, they could sign up to make an appointment or just stop by the counselor's office."

"That's what my class did, too, so I went with them."

"What were some of the stories?"

"Chelsea Parker told us about one of their track meets. She was in one of the same races and Summer's starting position was right behind her. You know how they start some of the races in starting blocks so they're kind of crouched over with their bum up in the air?"

Nicole rolled her eyes at that with her *yes, Captain Obvious* expression since she was on the track team.

Jennifer smiled inwardly as she caught it out of the corner of her eye but just nodded her affirmation for Matthew's benefit.

"Well, she was ahead of Summer once the race started but could tell Summer was gaining on her so started running faster. It happened one more time before the race was over. Chelsea won the race and when Summer came over to congratulate her, she told Chelsea she wasn't just trying to beat her. She was trying to catch up so she could tell her not to bend over again because the seam of Chelsea's shorts had split. Everyone cracked up at that. Even Chelsea."

As Matt was telling the story, a grin broke out on Nicole's face and by the end of the story she was laughing out loud.

"I remember that race! She was mortified when she found out and realized she could have been flashing anyone who was watching. Coach Kennedy teased her that maybe she should make those her lucky shorts and Summer should run behind her from then on because it was the first race that Chelsea won! Once she realized he was trying to tease her so she wouldn't be embarrassed and no one was trying to make fun of her, she thought it was funny, too."

Jennifer and Matt joined in the laughter and Jennifer knew in that moment her children would be okay.

"I'm so glad to hear you can have those happy memories. What happened to Summer and losing her at such a young age will be with you always and grieving is normal, but remembering the good times helps to move on. You don't need to feel like you have to always be sad or feel guilty when you laugh when you remember the silly times."

"Gee, Mom, maybe you should be a grief counselor."

Jennifer knew Matt's comment was a typical teenage remark and another Captain Obvious moment. She returned his smile and raised her hands palms up.

"Okay, okay, I get it."

Matthew picked his backpack up from the floor beside him where he'd placed it when he sat at the table. Removing a paper from inside the backpack, he handed it to Jennifer. "I almost forgot, they're starting a committee to do a memorial for Summer and asking parents to be volunteers."

Jennifer read the announcement about the committee. It was being headed by Rebecca McCormick, one of the math teachers at the high school. The first meeting was to be held on Friday at six pm. Jennifer knew Rebecca from parent teacher conferences and had always been struck by how well she interacted with her students. She was demanding, but fair and the kids respected her.

The Quilt Club was already honoring Summer with their quilt projects, but this would be another way for her to do her part. She debated about adding another responsibility to her calendar but knew it was something she had to do and would make the time to at least attend the meeting to learn what was being planned. She could decide then whether it was something she would go all-in for.

"I think I'll go to the meeting and find out more about it. Thanks for giving this to me so soon," she said, smiling at Matthew.

His face widened in a grin. It was an inside joke stemming from his tendency to forget to pass along announcements until right before an event was happening.

"I made brownies. Would either of you like some?"

"Yes!!" they both said at once.

After Jennifer got the plate of brownies along with glasses of milk for Matthew and Nicole and coffee for herself, they spent the next half hour discussing more pleasant topics about the first day of school. Life was almost back to its usual routine.

CHAPTER EIGHT

~

*J*ennifer walked up the flight of granite steps and through the heavy wooden doors into the lobby of Matthew and Nicole's high school where the committee meeting was to be held. She glanced around at the people already milling around in the lobby and more coming in behind her who looked like they may have come for the same reason.

If they're all here for the committee meeting, this is going to be a huge success.

She took the notice out of her purse scanning through the page to find the section where it mentioned the room she should report to. Spotting another parent she recognized standing near the trophy case, she walked over.

"Hi, Marianne, are you here for the memorial committee meeting, too?"

"Oh, hi, Jennifer. Yes. I was double-checking the room number. Looks like it's in Room 220. I still can't believe this has happened."

"It's a parent's worst nightmare. That may be a cliché, but I can't imagine anything worse happening to a parent than losing a child."

"I agree. They haven't identified the driver yet, have they?"

"Not yet."

Jennifer noticed the lobby was beginning to empty.

"We should probably go up to the room. Looks like it's quite a turnout and we might not find a seat otherwise."

They followed three other parents up the stairs and down the hallway to the room. She'd been here countless times both in her own school career and that of her children's and nearly every time the same thought struck her.

Why is it the classroom walls in all schools of a certain age are painted the same shade of sickly green? Do they get some sort of discount because no one else wants it?

At least fifteen other parents had already taken a seat and the room was filling up fast. Had they waited even another five minutes, Jennifer's concern about finding somewhere to sit would have been a reality. As it was, they were lucky to take the last two seats next to each other.

"This takes me back," Jennifer said to Marianne as she looked around the room. The desks were new and there was a whiteboard in addition to a chalkboard from the time when she'd been a student, but otherwise it brought back a sense of nostalgia of her years there. "I've been here for parent-teacher conferences when it's just the parent and teacher in the room, but this is the first time I've volunteered for a committee. Having all the seats filled is making it seem like we're back in class."

Marianne chuckled. "You're right, it does remind me of that. Did you attend this high school, too?"

"I did. How about you? Which high school did you go to?"

Marianne was about to answer but the sound of hands clapping at the front of the room signaled the meeting was being called to order and the room quieted.

"Thank you all for coming tonight. I'm grateful to see such an outpouring of support. For those of you who don't know me, my name is Rebecca McCormick and I teach Algebra I and II. I've been teaching at this school for the past ten years. I knew Summer and can't begin to tell you what a loss it is for our school community to not have her here. I want this memorial to be as special as she was. I thought it would be more efficient to break down into subcommittees to make sure all the details are handled with as little demand on your time as possible. I know we all have busy lives. Since we have such a big group, that's going to work out well. I'm going to pass around sign-up sheets for the various duties and if anyone thinks of something I didn't cover, let me know. I don't think we'll need anyone to serve on more than one of the subcommittees so if you would pick just one, that would be great. Please be sure to add your phone number and email address in case I have to get in touch in between meetings. Does anyone have any questions so far?"

"How often will we be meeting?" someone in the back asked.

"I plan to do an in-person meeting of the entire committee every week, but that might be changed once we have more of a sense of the details we'll need to address and the progress we're making. I'll leave it up to the various sub-committees to decide how often they'll want to meet."

"When will the memorial be held?" another parent asked.

"I've spoken with Principal Jackson, and we've set October fifteenth as the date. We thought it best not to delay it too far into the school year. It will be held in the school's auditorium followed by a reception in the cafeteria. I know that may not seem like a lot of time, but as long as we all stay focused, this should come together by then."

There were no other questions and the only sound in the room was the shuffling of the sign-up sheets for the sub-committees as they were passed around the room. By the time they got to Jennifer, she was surprised to see how evenly distributed the numbers of volunteers were for each of the tasks. She added her name to the Publicity sub-committee sign-up and passed the sheets on to the woman sitting in front of her, who was the last one to complete her selection. Ms. McCormick collected the forms and looked through them before addressing the room.

"I think we're off to a good start! Does anyone have anything else they'd like to add?"

Jennifer had been on the fence about mentioning the quilt club's idea but figured it couldn't hurt so raised her hand, realizing she was still in student mode by using the gesture instead of just speaking up.

"This may not go with the memorial service being done by the school, but my quilt club has decided to make quilts to donate to Project Linus in Summer's memory. If anyone is interested in participating or would like more information, let me know."

"Would you tell us what Project Linus is for those of us who don't know?" Rebecca asked.

"Oh, sure. It's an organization which collects donations of quilts or blankets and gives them to needy children. In addition to quilts, they can also be knit or crocheted but they must be handmade. I forgot to mention my quilt club is choosing designs for the blankets with the name summer in them but that's not a requirement."

"I'd be interested in donating one," one of the women spoke up.

"Me, too," a few others joined in.

"Would you be willing to head up that project?" Rebecca asked. "It would mean an extra duty in addition to what you've already signed up for."

"Of course, I don't mind at all. My quilt club is planning to do this anyway and I'm sure the other members would be happy to pitch in to help me."

"That's wonderful. Would all of those who said they'd like to donate a blanket please stay behind and give your contact information to Jennifer. Unless anyone else has a question, let's call it a night." She paused a moment to give an opportunity for anyone else to speak but the room was quiet. "In that case, thank you everyone. We'll meet back here next week at the same time."

"I wish I could help, but my needlework skills are nonexistent. I'll see you next week." Marianne waved her goodbye to Jennifer and followed the others leaving the room.

Once the room had emptied of everyone except those who had volunteered to make a quilt or blanket, Jennifer asked for their names and contact information and gave them the website address for the Project Linus organization to find the details for their requirements for donations. Her footsteps echoed as she walked down the hallway in the now mostly empty school. *I'm glad I came tonight.* She felt a sense of purpose knowing she was part of this group of volunteers who came together to honor Summer and help heal those she'd left behind. Ideas for how the quilts could be displayed for everyone to see were running through her head and her excitement about the project grew. She couldn't wait to let the Quilt Club know about the extra donations.

CHAPTER NINE

I had no idea there were so many quilt patterns with the name summer! The internet search Jennifer thought would take ten to fifteen minutes turned into ninety before she settled on one that felt like the perfect fit for her project. It had just the right balance of design, fabric choices, and challenge factor to make it interesting. She had even been able to find enough material in her stash to sew it without a trip to the quilt shop; not something that happened often.

I can't wait to share this with the ladies! Her enthusiasm was back today. She had the pattern decision and news about the additional blankets the memorial committee would be donating to share with the group.

The printer ran through its warmup preparations of clicks, beeps, and hums before finally spitting out the instructions she'd downloaded. Taking it from the output tray, she added it to the other sewing supplies she would need to take with her that night and packed them into the wheeled case she used to take her sewing machine to the meetings. The casserole she'd made earlier in the day was in the fridge. All David would have to do was warm it up for himself and the kids once they got home. They had already become immersed in after school activities which made everyone eating at the same time during the week a challenge. She and David made it non-negotiable Sunday dinner would be with everyone in attendance, and no phones or other electronic devices would be allowed at the table. They tried as much as possible to keep up during the week and Jennifer had set up a message center in the kitchen to make it convenient for everyone. It had a large whiteboard for each member of the household to write their schedules for the week. There was also a basket for the kids to put any papers requiring a parent's signature, or information they should at least be aware of. It had taken a while to come up with a system that worked, the biggest challenge of which was getting everybody to *use* the whiteboard and basket. Once it finally clicked for everyone that using it benefited them, life had become much easier.

"Jen, I'm home," David called out to her.

"I'm downstairs getting ready to go to the Cozy Quilts meeting, but I'll be right up to say goodbye."

She found David in their bedroom changing from his office attire into his jeans and tee shirt.

"How was your day?" she asked.

"Mostly good. I got a call from Debbie and Roger Williams to set up an appointment next week to file a claim for the life insurance policy they had for Summer. If there's any way you could be at the meeting, it would be a big help. I think it would put them more at ease. You have a way of making people comfortable even during the difficult situations… and I'm not saying that just because *I'm* the one who will be having a rough time with it."

She smiled to let him know she understood.

"Of course, just put it…"

"… on the whiteboard," he finished, grinning.

"I made a mac and cheese casserole for you and the kids. It's in the fridge and you can each heat it up in the microwave when you're ready."

"Thanks, hon. I appreciate that and I have no doubt the kids will, too."

He tried, but David wasn't known for his cooking skills. He took the teasing he received in stride, though.

"I better get going. I'll see you later," she said and gave him a kiss on the cheek.

"Have fun!"

"Thanks, I plan to."

She went into the kitchen to get the dessert she had made for the potluck supper and put everything in the car. Ten minutes later she was at Eva's house and reversed the process.

CHAPTER TEN

"You look like you're doing better this week," Eva noted when Jennifer arrived.

"I am. The shock has worn off and the kids seem to be handling it well. Having the grief counselors on site the first couple of days after school started had to have helped. If you wouldn't mind taking my food, I'll put my machine and supplies in your sewing room and be right back."

"Everyone is out in the screen room, but we didn't want to start serving the appetizers until you arrived. Annalise is checking with Sharon. She's not here yet but Annalise thought she was planning to come."

Almost as if on cue, the doorbell rang.

"Speak of the devil," Eva said when she opened the door to let Sharon in, grinning to let her know she was teasing. "You may have received a text from Annalise wondering if you were coming tonight."

"I'm so sorry. Am I late?" Sharon asked, a concerned look on her face.

"No, no. She wasn't sure if you were still able to make it since she hadn't heard any baby news. Jennifer just got here, too. You two go put your things away and I'll take the food. I'll let Annalise know you're here."

Sharon's older daughter was due to have her baby any day. It was her first grandchild and to say she was excited would have been a gross understatement.

Seating had never been assigned at the banquet tables Eva had set up for the members to use as their sewing station, but they each had gravitated organically to the same spots each week.

"Hey, Sharon. I'm guessing it means that Jessica still hasn't had the baby since you're here."

"Not yet. The doctor promises it will be soon, though."

They maneuvered their rolling sewing cases to their preferred locations. Without even being aware it was happening, they worked in synchrony as they performed the steps of setting up their stations. Sewing machines were pulled out of the cases, foot pedals were plugged into the power strips and lastly, their current works in progress and tools of the trade. Jennifer waited while Sharon put the finishing touches on her setup, looking around the room at the colorful displays of fabrics on each table. A smile came to her face as she thought about all the children who would be the beneficiaries of their quilts.

"I think I'm done. Ready to join the others?"

"I'm ready!" Jennifer replied.

As they stepped into the screened room, they were greeted with invitations to join the group. The warmth of the day lingered on this early September day and everyone was enjoying the opportunity to take advantage of the weather and time spent outside for as long as possible before the brisk autumn temperatures settled in. A cooler filled with ice and an assortment of water, plain and fizzy, and soft drinks was set up in a corner of the room. On the table were pitchers of lemonade and iced tea and a stack of paper cups. Jennifer and Sharon selected a drink and picked an empty seat.

"Paul let me know he won't be able to make it tonight. He forgot at the last meeting that he and Nicki had other plans, so it's just us. I told him not to worry about his food contribution since it was a side dish and we already have another one, so we can serve the appetizers and do our catching up," Eva said once everyone was together.

The appetizers and drinks were the traditional first part of the meeting which began with everyone telling the others what they'd been doing since the last time they met.

"I'll help you with those," Annalise offered, following Eva to the kitchen.

Eva and Annalise returned carrying one tray with the appetizers and another with plates and utensils which they placed on the table along with the cold beverages.

"I promised myself this week I'm not going to fill up on appetizers first, but I'm not sure I can keep that promise. This looks amazing." Sarah took a plate and began filling it with crudités, fruits, and a helping of the baked brie and crackers.

"How is Jessica holding up?" Annalise asked Sharon once they had all returned to their seats.

"Pretty much as expected. She wants it over. NOW. She was so disappointed last week when it turned out to be false labor. Let's just say it didn't help improve her cranky mood. I think Scott is almost as anxious as Jessica to have the baby arrive so his wife will be back to her usual sunny disposition."

"He has no idea, does he? They'll both be so exhausted that first month, being cranky from lack of sleep will be their normal," Jennifer said.

Although only Jennifer and Sharon had had the experience first-hand, everyone understood and joined in on the joke.

"Have you learned anything more about the accident or how it happened?" Sarah asked.

"I had a chance to talk to Karen LeBlanc after our meeting last week. I think I already told you she's the one who witnessed it happen and called 911. From what she told me, the car drifted onto the shoulder and Summer didn't have time to get out of the way. The driver stopped right afterwards but didn't even get out of the car to check on Summer. They just drove off. I don't understand how anyone could do that. How can they live with themselves knowing they may have killed someone?"

"It's truly hard to imagine," Eva agreed.

"You would have to be pretty cold-hearted to just drive away," Sarah said.

"Or scared," Annalise said. "I suspect there's more to this and the driver has a reason for not reporting it to the police. The only explanation I can think of is they were afraid this will lead to jail time for them. I'm not saying that's an excuse because there is no excuse, no matter what the consequences would be for them, but it's one possibility for why they still haven't come forward."

"I can see your point," Jennifer said. "It's got to catch up to them eventually, though. Either someone will be able to identify them or their car, or the guilt will be too much to continue hiding the truth of what happened."

The room quieted as they each considered those possibilities. Jennifer was the first to break the silence.

"I have something else to share with you. Rebecca McCormick, one of the math teachers at the high school, has started a committee to plan a memorial service for Summer to be held on October fifteenth. I volunteered for the sub-committee to do publicity for the event. I mentioned what we were doing about donating quilts and three other women said they'd like to donate one, too. It gave me the idea to put this out to the public in case others in the community might want to be a part of it. I was hoping Paul would be here tonight, but I can give him a call or drop into Quilting Essentials to ask if they would put a poster up in the store to advertise it. I wondered if any of you would be willing to help me coordinate the donations?"

"What a fantastic idea!" Sarah said. "There wouldn't be much for us to do, would there? I mean, the quilt shop is already a drop off site for donations."

"That's a good point," Jennifer said. "I don't want to create more work for them either. I'll ask them if they would be okay with it when I speak with Paul, or even Evelyn. Talking to Evelyn might be a better idea since she's the owner of the shop. My thought was to have the quilts be brought to the high school first so we can display them at the memorial service. That way Evelyn wouldn't have to find space for them until after that. I'm going to print out a sign-up sheet with instructions and a space for anyone donating a blanket to write out their name and address so the committee can send a thank you. If anyone can help me with those and the quilt display, that would be great."

"Sounds like a good plan, and I'm more than happy to help out with both of those," Eva said, and the others nodded their agreement.

"Have you thought about having labels made for the donations that would say they're made in Summer's memory?" Annalise asked.

"I hadn't, but if Project Linus allows it, that would be a great idea. I'll check their website when I get home."

"Since you're on the Publicity Committee, I'd be happy to introduce you to Susan Reynolds at The Bangor News to get the word out. I think she might be interested in doing a story about the memorial and the quilt project," Annalise offered.

"That would be wonderful! Please do," Jennifer said. "I've been thinking about how to display the quilts on the night of the event but could use your advice as to whether you think it would work. It might depend on how many quilts are donated but at some of the quilt shows I've gone to they've pinned them to room dividers."

"I know exactly what you mean," Annalise said. "I think that could work. The quilts or blankets will probably all be small so you could have more than one on a panel."

"You'd need to rent the panels, wouldn't you?" Sarah asked.

"I'll have to check with the school to see if they have any, but we provide the insurance for one of the equipment rental companies in Bangor and I might be able to convince them to donate enough or at the very least give us a discount. If we have to pay for them, David and I can cover the cost."

"Is anyone else ready for the next course now?" Eva asked when that topic appeared to be finished.

"I shouldn't be after the way I pigged out on the appetizers, but my stomach is telling me otherwise," Sarah said.

"I resemble that remark," Annalise quipped.

The meeting progressed on its usual schedule and Jennifer left at the end of the evening energized and ready to get started on the next tasks for the memorial. It was by no means a substitute for Summer being gone, but perhaps the gesture of keeping her memory alive through the donation project would be a comfort to her parents.

CHAPTER ELEVEN

∼

The past couple of days there had been just a touch of a chill in the air prompting Jennifer to tackle the job of bringing out her cold weather clothes in anticipation of the change of seasons. This year she promised herself instead of just transferring them to her closet and bureau drawers, she would go through them first. She heard the muffled ringtone of her phone and looked around in confusion, not seeing it anywhere, before realizing it was buried under the piles of clothes on her bed. She began digging through the clothes but wasn't able to find it. When she finally reached the spot where she'd tossed it earlier, the ringing had stopped but there was a voice mail alert. Annalise had called to suggest getting together for lunch.

"I know we see each other at the quilt club meetings, but I'm thinking we need a girls' get-together that's not about quilting. I'll call Eva and Sarah and ask if they can come, too. Would you be available to come on Thursday at the diner? Give me a call when you can."

Jennifer checked the family calendar before returning the call, but it went straight to voice mail.

She must be on the phone with Eva or Sarah.

"Hey, Annalise. I got your message. Thursday should work for me. I'm free all day so I can work around everyone else's time schedule."

Putting the phone in her pocket this time, she went back to her sorting.

Fifteen minutes later Annalise called again.

"Eva can join us Thursday at noon, but Sarah has a big project due this week so won't be able to make it."

"Oh, that's too bad. I was looking forward to getting to know more about her. Maybe another time. I'll put it on my calendar and see you and Eva then."

Jennifer arrived at the Checkout Diner a little early on Thursday and parked next to Annalise's and Eva's cars in the parking lot. The aroma of coffee and burgers frying on the grill greeted her as she walked through the door and her stomach grumbled, reminding her she had missed breakfast that morning. The diner's interior was decorated in typical diner style with red vinyl upholstery on the booths' bench seating and Formica tabletops were situated to the left of the entrance. The red vinyl and Formica were repeated on the stools and long counter facing the entrance. The right side of the diner's seating area had tables and chairs, but the ladies preferred the booths. Looking in that direction, Jennifer found her friends seated at the last one in the row. She greeted Betty Jones, the diner's waitress and unofficial town crier as she passed by the lunch counter. If you wanted to find out what was going on in Glen Lake, Betty was the one who could tell you.

"I mentioned on the phone I'd like to get to know you better. I didn't bring a questionnaire, but I do have questions," Annalise said, grinning, once Jennifer had settled into her spot beside Eva. "Did you grow up here? Do you have family nearby?"

"I grew up in Glen Lake and have only lived somewhere else for a couple years after I graduated from high school. When I told my mom and dad I didn't want to go to college, I thought they would blow a gasket. They couldn't understand that I needed a break from school and wanted to get out in the 'real world'," she said, using air quotes. "I went to work as a secretary in an insurance agency right after I graduated high school but compromised with my parents by taking a couple business classes at night at the community college. Two of my girlfriends and I decided to get an apartment together in Bangor. We thought we were so grown-up living in the city. We had no idea how sheltered our lives had been." Jennifer chuckled at the memory. "Our parents weren't very happy about it at first but relented on the condition that we would have to cover all the expenses on our own and made us give them a budget. I think that was more for us than them so we would see how much it would really cost. They knew we were all wearing our rose-colored glasses when it came to what we were taking on. My parents paid for my college classes but everything else was on me."

"Smart parents. Better to be practical before you got in over your heads," Eva said.

"We got a major reality check when they pointed out all the expenses we hadn't thought about, but we were still able to have enough money left over so that we weren't making ourselves house poor. We found an apartment in a decent part of town and shopped thrift stores to furnish it. It was a lot of fun finding deals for things we needed. I had sewing skills even then so made pillows and curtains and some other home decorations. We were lucky that we all got along and were responsible about paying our share of the bills so no drama."

"You mentioned only living in the apartment a couple years. What changed?" Annalise asked.

"David," Jennifer replied, smiling. "He grew up in Glen Lake, too, so we knew each other all through school but we were just friends. My roommates and I were invited to a house-warming party another friend from high school was throwing and David had been invited, too. We ended up starting a conversation and then spent the rest of the party talking to each other. We realized there was a spark there and he asked me out. The rest is history. We got engaged when he was a junior at the University of Maine and I moved back with my parents until we got married the June after he graduated. We wanted to save money for a down payment for a house so my parents suggested that I should move back with them, although they did ask for a token rent. I didn't realize until later they were putting that money away for me and once David and I found a house we wanted shortly before we got married, they gave it back to help with the financing expenses. I have to admit I had complained to my friends about them asking for rent money especially after they were the ones who suggested I move back home. Even though they had no idea I'd been such a brat, they got an apology once they told me what they'd done."

Everyone chuckled at that confession.

"I kept working after David and I were married but once Matthew came along, I became a stay-at-home mom. Because I had worked for an insurance agency, I was able to help David out when he decided to start his own agency. Once both the kids were in school all day, I began to work at the agency part-time. He insisted on paying me a salary just like any other employee even though I didn't ask. It's been good for me to have my own money so I can support my habit of buying far too many quilting supplies."

"I wouldn't know anything about that," Eva said but rolled her eyes.

"After seeing your studio, I would never have guessed," Annalise played along, eliciting a laugh from Eva and Jennifer.

"Do you have any siblings?" Eva asked.

"Just a sister, Rosemary, who lives in southern Maine. She's married and has three kids, all about the same ages as Matt and Nicole."

"I remember you saying your parents live out-of-state," Annalise said.

"Yes, they got tired of Maine winters and moved to Florida a couple years ago. It worked out for us, too, as now we have a warm place to visit in the winter. We took the kids down last year during the February school vacation. The downside was coming back to two more months of winter."

They were interrupted by Betty bringing their lunch orders.

"Here you go, ladies. Give me a holler if you need anything else," she said and hurried off to attend to another table of customers.

"This was a wonderful idea, Annalise," Jennifer said. "I'm realizing I've missed having close female friends. Most of the friends I have revolve around the kids' school functions. Now that Matt and Nicole will be graduating soon, I know the reality is those friendships will likely drift apart without that connection. It's not that I don't like them, but the friendships have been more superficial than what I've felt with all of you."

"Turning forty brings about changes for a lot of women. It's when we find our voice," Eva said.

"I agree. I realized I was less willing to put my needs last and learned it was okay to say no. It didn't come easily at first because throughout my life I was a people pleaser," Annalise said.

"I know exactly what you mean!" Jennifer said, warming to the subject. "It's like a switch was flipped and one day I woke up thinking I don't have to do that anymore. It's okay to ask for things for myself."

Eva chuckled. "That may be one of several reasons for my divorce. Kenneth and I got married later in life, but I hadn't quite reached that stage of my evolution when we started dating. There came a point, though, when I wasn't willing to put up with a lot of things I'd been sweeping under the rug for years. We parted on amiable terms and I'm much happier now. Jim and I have an agreement we're a couple but living separately suits us both."

Jim Davis was a widower and had been Eva's partner for the past two years. Prior to his retirement, he worked as a Maine state trooper. He still maintained friendships through activities with police officers including a weekly poker night and police softball league. Those friendships and Jim's experience as a law enforcement officer had been helpful when the Cozy Quilts Club team had been working on the two murder cases they'd solved.

"That's so true about saying no and not feeling guilty about it anymore. If it hadn't been for knowing Summer, I don't think I would have joined the memorial committee. David got it right when he said most of the committees I've been on before were a lot of work for not a lot of reward. I think Rebecca is going to be an excellent coordinator. She's organized and I got the impression from our first meeting that she will keep us on track, but she won't micro-manage the sub-committees. The kids have always spoken highly of her. They say she's tough, but fair when it comes to grading and is willing to give help outside of classes if anyone is having a problem understanding the math concepts. I don't remember if I've mentioned she teaches Algebra at their high school."

"I think you did mention it when you first told us about the memorial committee. How is that going, by the way?" Eva asked.

"We have a lot to do, but I think we'll make it on time. A Facebook group has been set up as a way for the sub-committees to coordinate and post updates on their progress. I put together an announcement about Project Linus in case there's anyone else who wants to make a donation, and Rebecca made sure each homeroom had enough announcements for all the students to take a copy home. Before I forget again, I meant to thank you earlier, Annalise, for putting me in touch with Susan Reynolds.

We met a couple days ago and she's doing a piece about the event for The Bangor News. So far, I've had six people contact me to say they'd like to participate. It isn't a lot of time to make something but since the blankets can be smaller, it's more manageable. Which reminds me, I need to get busy with mine. I started it using fabric from my stash but changed my mind because it just didn't feel like Summer to me after I saw what it looked like once I had one block put together. So, you know what I'll be doing," she smiled.

"Sounds like you have a trip to Quilting Essentials in your future and you don't need to be a psychic to predict that," Annalise teased in a self-deprecating way. After all, she was one.

CHAPTER TWELVE

∼

"Mmmm. Something smells good." David called up to Jennifer from downstairs when he got home from work and parked the car in the garage. "I've got something to tell you after I change out of my work clothes." A few minutes later he joined Jennifer in the kitchen.

"There's a fresh pot of coffee and I made a batch of cookies if you don't think it will ruin your dinner. What's the news?"

After so many years of living together, Jennifer and David moved around each other as though their motions were choreographed. Without either of them missing a beat, he filled a coffee mug, added half and half from the carton in the refrigerator, and helped himself to two cookies before sitting at the kitchen table while she gathered the ingredients to make a salad and took them to the counter beside the sink.

"There's a rumor circulating around town that Theresa Blackstone remembered seeing a silver four-door sedan, with a broken headlight and dented fender on the passenger side, pass her driveway as she was walking to her mailbox. She thought she'd heard tires screeching as though a car had braked hard not long before she saw the car but had been inside, so wasn't positive about that detail. She hadn't consciously done it, but once the car passed her, she had turned to look more closely to try to see the driver. By then the car was already far enough away that she only saw the back of their head. She could tell it was a female and thought it might have been Linda Martin from her hair color and style and because she drives the same type of car."

"Didn't she hear the sirens from the police and ambulance?" Jennifer asked. "She lives just on the other side of the curve in the road where the accident happened."

"She said it had registered in her subconscious, but she didn't report what she'd seen right away. It was long enough between when she saw the car and she heard the sirens that she didn't connect it with Summer. She also never considered that someone would just drive off after hitting a person. It wasn't until she was listening to the news the next day that she put two and two together."

"Are the police going to question Linda?"

"I'm sure they will if for no other reason than to eliminate her. You probably remember she had a couple DUI citations on her record from a few years ago so that would factor in, too."

"Yes, I remember," Jennifer said. "She's been sober since then, though. She's shared with me that she attends AA meetings and hasn't had a drink since she had the last DUI violation."

"I hope for her sake that is still true, but it wouldn't be the first time someone has relapsed."

"So do I. Not just for her sobriety but having left the scene of a fatal accident is even worse as far as I'm concerned," Jennifer said.

"I agree."

EVA AND JIM were at the Checkout Diner that same evening and news of the witness account was making the rounds there as well.

"Did you hear that Theresa Blackstone might have identified the driver who killed Summer Williams?" Betty Jones asked them when she came to take their orders.

"No! Do you know who it was?" Eva asked.

"She wasn't sure because she only saw the back of their head, but she thought it might have been Linda Martin. It was the same color and type of car the news had reported that fled the scene. And the car had a busted headlight and a dent in the fender." Her tone implied that was all that needed to be said on the subject to prove the case.

"Why didn't she report it right away?" Jim asked.

"The story I got was that Theresa didn't know about the accident until the next day. It was only then she realized it might have been the car that drove away. She'd been walking down her driveway to check her mailbox and just happened to see it going by and the damage to the fender and headlight caught her attention."

"Do you know if the police have questioned Linda?"

"Not yet. It would be good to finally have the driver identified and arrested but I hope for Linda's sake it isn't her. I would have had an easier time a year ago believing it was her because of her drinking problems, but she's been doing so well since then. I can't imagine she would have fallen off the wagon from the times I've seen her, but I guess you just never know," Betty said.

Not having anything new to add to the conversation, she moved on to her usual business of serving customers.

"Do you know Linda?" Eva asked Jim.

"Only in passing, but I would agree with Betty's assessment that it doesn't fit with Linda's sobriety over the past year. Not to say that driving under the influence was the reason the person who struck Summer fled the scene. There might have been another explanation."

"That's true. I think people are more likely to go in the direction of alcohol being a factor because it's so difficult to believe anyone would have done it with a clear mind and then just drove away."

Before Jim had an opportunity to comment, Betty returned to their booth with their drinks and the conversation moved on to more pleasant subjects.

As they were driving home, Jim abruptly slowed down.

"What's wrong?" Eva asked. She had been lost in her own thoughts but focused her attention now, first looking around at the trees on one side of the road and then to the house on the other. It was dark now, but Eva couldn't see anything that warranted their sudden deceleration.

"That's Linda Martin's house. All the lights are out, and it looks like no one is home. The lamppost at the end of her driveway has always been on when I've passed by here at night." Jim didn't offer any other explanation but accelerated the car and continued on their way.

Eva picked up on what he must be thinking and felt a sense of dread come over her. Was it more than just a rumor that Linda could be responsible for Summer's death?

CHAPTER THIRTEEN

∼

Jennifer had the morning off and decided it was a good time to start her second attempt of her quilt project for the Project Linus donation. Her publicity committee duties of putting the word out to the community had been keeping her busy or she would have started sooner. In addition to buying fabric, she needed to speak with Evelyn Jackson at Quilting Essentials about all the donations that would eventually be coming to her shop. She'd meant to do it sooner, but time had gotten away from her. She was still hoping Evelyn would give her permission to put up a poster and leave a stack of sign-up sheets to hand out to customers.

As always, the rainbow of colors and patterns of the fabrics in the shop started her creative juices flowing as soon as she stepped over the threshold. It was a weekday morning so there wasn't much activity in the shop. Luck was with her as Evelyn was at the checkout counter at the front of the store and not with a customer.

"Good morning, Evelyn! You're just the person I wanted to see," Jennifer said.

"Hi, Jennifer! I've been expecting you. Paul told me about the Cozy Quilts Club's plans to donate quilts in Summer's memory."

"That's one of the reasons why I'm here, because the project has expanded since I last talked to Paul. You probably already know that Summer's high school is planning a memorial service on October fifteenth. I volunteered to serve on the Publicity Committee and when I told the group about the Project Linus quilts, I had more offers for donations."

"That's terrific! I know the organization will be thrilled to have them."

"But wait, there's more," Jennifer said with a smile, knowing her words were an old catchphrase.

Evelyn chuckled in response. "Okay, what more is there?"

"Susan Reynolds interviewed me to do a human interest story about the memorial plans and I mentioned this project along with what the high school has in the works. I asked Susan to hold off on printing the story until I had a chance to speak with you, though, so you wouldn't be blindsided. We're asking for all donations to first be brought to the high school so we can display them at the memorial service. I'll bring them here after that, so you won't have to be taking them in piecemeal. I wondered, though, if you would mind handing out sign-up sheets to your customers? I've printed a form with instructions and a link to the Project Linus website if people have any questions about what they'll accept for donations. It also has a spot for donors to fill in their name and contact information so we can send thank you notes. If you're okay with it, I'd like to have Susan mention that they can pick up a donation form here."

"Of course, I don't have any problem with that and appreciate you already have the forms prepared. Do you have them with you today?"

"I do. Just one more favor. Would you be willing to display a poster about the donations and the memorial celebration either in your window or somewhere else inside the shop?"

"I'd be happy to. Summer was a great kid and we're happy to do anything we can to honor her."

"Thank you so much! I'll be right back with the poster and donation forms. I thought you would be okay with it, but didn't want to just assume," Jennifer said and left to retrieve them from her car. Evelyn was waiting at the checkout when she returned and had brought out a box to collect the donor forms.

"That will be perfect," Jennifer said when Evelyn showed her the box. "Here are the forms for donors to fill out," she said handing them to Evelyn. "And here's the poster."

"I can put a mention of this in our newsletter, too. It's not a long time to make a quilt but I can suggest some easy patterns that would sew up quickly in the same article."

"That's a great idea! Thank you so much. It's not required, but at the Cozy Quilts meeting, we decided to pick designs that have the name summer in them."

"Paul didn't tell me that, but I'll be sure to put that in the newsletter, too, and see if I can find patterns for some of those to suggest."

"You're the best! I'll let Susan know it's okay to go ahead with her piece and it should be out in the next day or two. On the one hand, I hope it doesn't make a lot of work for you, but on the other hand, I hope it's a success and we get a good response."

"Don't worry about making work for us. You've already done the hard part. All we need to do is hand out the forms for people to fill in."

"Speaking of a donation, that's the other reason why I came here today. I wanted to buy new material to make my project."

Paul Taylor had come from the back of the shop to join their conversation and Evelyn filled him in about the forms and box she had labeled to collect them.

"There's been some gossip about Linda Martin possibly being the driver," Paul said.

"That's what Dave told me last night, too," Jennifer said.

"Do you really think it could have been her?" Evelyn asked.

"We really shouldn't jump to conclusions, but I don't think it could be Linda. Silver four-door sedans are very common so just because she drives one, doesn't mean it was her. And from what Dave was told, Theresa Blackstone didn't get a good look at the driver. She only saw the back of the woman's head so it could have been anyone," Jennifer cautioned.

"You're right," Paul agreed. "The police will get to the bottom of it but in the meantime, it's not fair to speculate one way or the other."

"Agreed," Evelyn added. "How about we get back to what you came here for; buying fabric to make a quilt. Is there anything I can help you find?"

Jennifer said a silent thank you they hadn't contributed to the rumor mill. Linda Martin deserved to be considered innocent unless proven otherwise.

"I'm looking for shades of blue and green, and maybe small floral prints. They make me think of Summer and I have a pattern picked out with the name summer in it so would fit with our theme. I brought it with me so I'd have the yardages I'll need," Jennifer said, removing the printout of the pattern from her reusable shopping bag and handing it to Evelyn.

"We should have just what you need in this section," Evelyn said leading the way and Jennifer followed.

CHAPTER FOURTEEN

Jennifer's heart went out to them when Debbie and Roger Williams arrived at David's office. They both had dark circles under their eyes which even Debbie couldn't hide with makeup. Their faces were drawn, and it was obvious they were both lacking sleep. Their demeanor was what Jennifer had expected to be shown by parents who had lost a child, but it was still shocking to see it manifested before her. She went to Debbie and wrapped her in her arms as they clung together, both trying not to cry as one gave and the other received emotional support. They broke the embrace in unspoken mutual agreement and Debbie dabbed at her eyes with the tissue she already had in her hand.

"I'm hesitant to say this as I suspect you must be tired of hearing it, but I truly am so sorry about Summer and that we are meeting today under these circumstances. She was a beautiful young woman, inside and out," Jennifer said.

"Please have a seat," David said after shaking their hands

and gestured toward the seats opposite his desk and took his own once they had been seated. Jennifer had placed another chair to David's left for herself thinking it might help support him through this difficult meeting.

"How are you both holding up?" David asked. "I mean honestly, not just the polite answer."

Roger and Debbie exchanged glances before Roger answered.

"We're getting through the days, just barely. Everyone has been so kind, and we're truly grateful. The first few days were a blur between the shock of the news and then making the funeral arrangements. It might sound odd, but that time might have been easier than it is now. Once the funeral was over, it's as though we lost our compass. Before that we had distractions to keep us from reality settling in but now..." his voice trailed off.

Debbie picked up where he'd left off.

"People are around for those days right after a death but then go on living their own lives, as they should. That's when it really hits you, when you are past those first few days. It's not something we'd thought about until it happened to us. We know this is the kind of event that can destroy families. We've heard about how marriages can fall apart, and parents forget about their living children, and we don't want that to happen to us."

"How is Emma doing?" Jennifer asked.

Emma was Summer's younger sister. She was in the same class, but Nicole hadn't mentioned anything about Emma since Summer's death.

"She's trying to be brave, but I'm worried about her. The grief counselor at school gave us the name of a family counselor and we have an appointment scheduled next week," Debbie said.

"That's a really good idea. It sounds like you are all committed to working through this. There's no doubt in my mind that with time you'll make it to the other side of this as a family," David said.

"That's the plan," Roger said, his voice shaky but determined.

"Before we move on, I want to thank you for what you're doing with the memorial, Jennifer. The quilt project is such a wonderful idea. I think Summer would be touched. She loved kids and having those donated in her name to an organization like Project Linus is a perfect tribute," Debbie said.

"Thank you. Eva Perkins at my quilt club was the one who came up with the idea, so I can't take credit for it. It was originally just going to be the six members of the Cozy Quilts Club donating. When I mentioned it at the first committee meeting and had more people volunteer, I realized it might be something the entire community would want to participate in. We're getting quite a few sign-ups so if everyone comes through, we should have a lot of donations. We plan to display them in the cafeteria where they'll be having the reception after the service itself. I hope you'll be able to make it so you can see them all."

"I wouldn't miss it," Debbie said, smiling for the first time since they had arrived, and Jennifer knew it was heartfelt.

"Have the police given you any updates?" David asked. "There's a rumor going around town about Linda Martin possibly being involved but I hope that isn't true."

"It isn't," Roger replied. "The police did question her and as it turns out, her car had recently been in a minor fender bender, but her tire treads didn't match the skid marks left on the road. Her tires weren't new, so it wasn't like she had replaced them recently. Plus, she had a solid alibi as to her whereabouts for that day."

"I'm really happy to hear that. Linda has worked so hard on her sobriety and rebuilding her reputation. Hopefully that message will get out quickly so people will stop spreading the rumor it was her," Jennifer said.

"I hope so, too," Roger agreed. "We're doing our part when we can. Maybe someone can get Betty Jones on it. That would get the word out." He grinned letting Jennifer and David know he wasn't saying this with malice. Everyone was aware that Betty was prone to gossip, but she never meant it to be malicious. It was her way of making small talk and seemed clueless that gossip wasn't the best way to do that.

"Maybe we should go to the Diner for dinner tonight and do our part to get Betty started on that," David said to Jennifer.

"You won't get any argument from me!"

David looked down at the paper on his desk and then slid it along with a pen toward Roger and Debbie so they could read it.

"This is the claim form for Summer's life insurance. We'll need a certified copy of her death certificate along with the completed form to send to the insurance company to file the claim. I'll give you a few minutes to look it over, but it should be self-explanatory."

Roger and Debbie sat silently reading the claim form before Roger reached for the pen and began filling it out.

"I brought a copy of the death certificate," Debbie said, reaching into her purse and removed it along with a packet of tissues. She pulled one out and dabbed at her eyes and then set her shoulders before looking up at Jennifer and David. "Roger and I have talked about what we want to do with the money from the policy and decided to set up a scholarship in Summer's name for kids who can't afford to go to the camp she worked at. She loved working with the kids and planned to keep doing it even while she was in college."

"What a nice idea. Summer would be so pleased," Jennifer said. Her already high regard for the Williams went up a notch.

"The check will be in your names since that's how the beneficiary designation was set up, but I assume you have an attorney who can walk you through setting up the scholarship fund," David added.

"We do. We've already been in touch and they're putting

together the paperwork," Roger said as he finished filling out and signing the claim form before passing it to Debbie for her signature.

"I think that's it," David said when Debbie returned the pen and paperwork to him. "If there's anything we can do for you, please let us know, and I mean that. The people in Glen Lake look out for each other which is one of the reasons Jennifer and I have stayed here."

Debbie smiled in acknowledgement.

"I agree. I'm not sure we could have made it through those first days if it hadn't been for the support from the community," she said and then turned to Roger. "Are you ready to go or is there anything else I forgot to ask?"

"No, that should be everything we needed," Roger said and stood to leave. Jennifer came to Debbie once she'd stood and gave her another hug as David and Roger shook hands.

After they'd left the office, Jennifer let out a sigh.

"I don't know if I would be doing as well as they are. I think I'm going to talk to Matt and Nicky about keeping an eye on Emma."

"Good idea. They've been friends all through school and Nicky has invited her for sleepovers before so it wouldn't be completely out of left field for her to suddenly be paying attention."

"That's a good point. If Emma thought Summer's death was the only reason Nicky or Matt were speaking to her more, that might be even worse."

"Do you know if the kids have anything going on later today? We could all go to the Checkout for dinner or bring them back a pizza."

"I'll text them just in case they didn't put it on the calendar, but I don't remember seeing anything. They should be out of classes by now." After sending the text, she didn't have long to wait for an answer letting Jennifer know they would like a pepperoni pizza. "We have a request for pizza, but they would rather have it as takeout so it's just you and me. Does this count as a date night?"

David smiled. "That works for me."

CHAPTER FIFTEEN

Jennifer retrieved the empty plastic tote she found in the garage earlier and put it in the trunk of her car to take to the high school office. They had agreed to collect any donations that came in but Jennifer wanted to have a clean tote with a lid to put them in so they would be protected until it was time for the memorial service. She also needed to take more donation forms in for the office staff to hand out. They had already given out the dozen Jennifer had brought in the week before. She hadn't expected such a large response to the project. Chances were not everyone who took a form would donate a blanket but if even half of them did, Project Linus would be receiving a generous supply to give to children who needed them. Knowing that made the extra time she was putting in worth every second.

Classes were dismissed for the day when she arrived, but the office was open until four pm. The school's parking lot had emptied out of the majority of the cars that had been there during class times and she found a spot near the door, which was why she had put off coming until later in the day. It was a perfect autumn day with a bright blue sky and sunshine making it still tee shirt weather. She could make out the sounds of teams practicing on the athletic field and made a mental note to check the calendar when she got home to see when Nicole's next track meet and Matthew's soccer games were. Sometimes the schedules conflicted, so she'd have to make sure she and David coordinated so each of the kids would have at least one of their parents attending.

The sound of her shoes clicking on the tiles as she walked into the lobby echoed in the empty halls. With tote and sign-up forms in hand, she made her way to the office situated to the left of the lobby. Rebecca McCormick was in the office speaking with Gretchen Fields, the principal's secretary.

"Hello, Jennifer. Is the tote for the quilt donations?" Gretchen asked.

"Yes. I thought it might be better than a cardboard box. I brought some more sign-up sheets, too," she said to Gretchen before turning to Rebecca.

"I know we have a committee meeting later this week, Ms. McCormick, but is there anything I should know now? I'm planning to have at least a draft of a newsletter finished tonight to send out from the Publicity Committee. After you've had a chance to approve it first, of course, but there still time to add it in."

"Please call me Becky. At least while there aren't any kids around," Rebecca said, smiling. "I can't think of anything at the moment but if I do, I'll send you an email. And I just want you to know what a great job you've been doing getting the word out. The article that was in The Bangor News was terrific. I was going to tell you this at the regular meeting but since you're here, I can tell you now. The article brought the memorial service to the attention of Channel 6, and they contacted me about doing an interview. I'd like to have you be a part of that but didn't want to commit until I had a chance to ask if you'd be willing to do it."

"Oh," Jennifer said, taken aback. "I've never been on TV before but if you think it would help and you'll be with me, I guess it would be okay."

"I was thinking the same thing about having someone else with me. They've given us three options for when they could schedule it here at school. I don't have those with me but can email you later. Any one of them worked for me so I'm happy to work around your schedule."

"Perfect! I'll let you know as soon as I have a chance to check with my husband and the kids."

"Have either of you heard any updates about the driver who hit Summer?" Gretchen asked.

Jennifer saw Rebecca's eyes flicker but just as quickly returned to normal. Thinking it was odd but that she must have imagined it, Jennifer turned to Gretchen.

"No one has told me anything new and I'm worried the police are running out of tips," she said.

"Me, either," Rebecca said.

"I hope they can find whoever it was soon. My husband and I met with her parents earlier this week. It broke my heart to see how this has affected them but having some closure and seeing the person brought to justice would go a long way for their healing."

"I couldn't agree more. And for Emma, too. She puts on a brave face and the other kids have been very supportive of her, but I think she's hiding a lot of pain," Gretchen said.

Jennifer considered mentioning that the Williams were setting Emma up with a counselor but realized that should remain confidential.

"Well, I should get back to my classroom and close it up for the day. I'll get those dates to you and see you at the committee meeting," Rebecca said before hurrying out of the room and down the hall to the stairway.

"I should get going, too," Jennifer said to Gretchen.

"Let me take those for you," Gretchen said, and Jennifer handed over the tote and forms.

"Thanks. If you need me to bring more, just let me know. I'll be happy to send them in with Matt or Nicky."

"I will," Gretchen said.

As Jennifer left to walk back to her car, her thoughts went back to Rebecca's reaction when Gretchen asked about the hit-and-run driver. There was something off about it, but she couldn't put her finger on what was bothering her. Her logical side argued that she was making far too much of it and the idea that Rebecca McCormick would be hiding something didn't make sense.

Was it possible she was protecting someone? That doesn't make sense either. Would she be doing all this for Summer if she knew who the driver was but didn't come forward with the information?

She stopped dead in her tracks. *Or worse, was she the driver?*

That possibility was unimaginable, and she chastised herself for even thinking it. There was no way Rebecca could have done that and then put on the charade of heading up the memorial service out of concern for Summer's memory.

All the way home, she kept replaying the conversation in the office in her head. That flicker of Rebecca's eyes and the way she scurried out of the office kept nagging at her. No matter how much she tried to dismiss it, the question wouldn't let go. *Is Rebecca involved?*

CHAPTER SIXTEEN

The Cozy Quilts Club was gathered for their regular meeting along with part-time members Sharon Ramos and Paul Taylor. Although the days were still warm, the nights cooled off quickly now, so they were inside instead of in her screened room where they had held their dinners during the summer months. Eva was wrapping up the leftovers from their potluck dinner into separate containers for each of them to take home.

Couldn't you at least just once *make one of those containers for me?* Reuben had left his cushion in the living room to join them in the kitchen and was now glaring at Eva.

"No, you cannot have one so just stop asking."

Sarah looked up from the kitchen sink where she was rinsing out her glass, her brows furrowed. She realized Eva was talking to Reuben, not her, when she saw him stand up and give Eva a scathing glance and a *meow* which Eva did not translate. The others lingering in the kitchen waiting for Eva and Sarah before beginning their projects, tried not to laugh at Reuben's drama queen departure.

"Tell us how it's going with the blanket donations you're getting," Eva asked Jennifer when they'd all moved into the sewing studio.

"It's going great! I had to take in more sign-up sheets at school earlier this week because they had run out. I took a tote in, too, to store them. I know not everyone who took a sign-up will donate a quilt or blanket but if they did, that would mean more than a dozen additional quilts for the cause."

"Did Susan Reynolds's article help?" Annalise asked.

"I don't have a way to know for sure, but I'm convinced it did. And it also prompted Channel 6 to ask if Rebecca and I would do an on-camera interview. Rebecca was in the office when I took the tote in and asked me if we could tape it next week."

"How exciting! Are you going to do it?" Sarah asked.

"I am since I would have Becky... she asked me to call her that... with me. The reporter is coming to school on Wednesday afternoon at three. I don't know when it will air but I'll let you know in case you want to watch it."

"Listen to you! You sound just like a TV personality talking about when it will air," Eva teased.

Jennifer blushed but played along. "Don't worry, I won't forget you when I'm a star."

That elicited laughter from everyone.

"Something happened when we were in the office, though. I'm not sure if I imagined it but when Gretchen Fields... she's the principal's secretary... asked if we'd heard any updates about the identity of the driver who killed Summer, I could have sworn there was something off in Becky's expression. Almost like she knew something but didn't want to talk about it. It passed so quickly, though, that I'm not one hundred percent sure. We both told Gretchen that we hadn't and then Becky left almost right after that claiming she had to close up her classroom." Jennifer hesitated, debating whether to mention it had crossed her mind that Rebecca might be the driver.

"Do you think she might be protecting someone?" Paul asked.

"That occurred to me. She has a good relationship with her students so she might be doing it for one of them although it seems like that would be contrary to her character. I suppose it could be that she's talking to the student and trying to convince them to turn themselves in."

"Am I remembering correctly that your kids told you there was a rumor going around that it might have been another member of the track team?" Sharon asked.

"Yes, they were saying it might be Lacey Daniels. She was jealous of Summer, but I don't think anyone seriously thought it was her despite the rumor. Even if they did, Lacey's mother put a stop to that quickly. She's a lawyer at one of the top firms in Bangor and has a reputation for being ruthless when it comes to defending her clients. Lacey had an airtight alibi for the day Summer was killed. She had to have her wisdom teeth removed, which is why she was absent the first day of school, too. From what Matt and Nicky told me, her mother came to Principal Jackson's office and demanded that he put out a statement that any rumors about Lacey were untrue and they should stop immediately, which he did. The last thing the school district needs is a defamation lawsuit."

"I hope it's not one of the students. That would be something that would be with them for the rest of their life even if it was an accident and they panicked and left the scene," Eva said.

No one spoke but everyone could sense their mutual agreement. Jennifer's internal debate continued, but she decided she wasn't ready to share her suspicions yet. She wasn't sure whether that was out of fairness to Rebecca because she had no evidence to prove it, or that speaking it aloud might make it true.

When no one had any more to offer on that subject, Eva switched topics.

"Why don't we finish up a few minutes earlier than usual and do a show and tell?" she suggested.

"Great idea! I'd love to see everyone's project," Annalise agreed.

Ninety minutes later Reuben stalked into the sewing room to Eva's spot.

Your alarm woke me up, he told Eva, obviously annoyed. *You left your phone in the dining room, and it's been blaring for the past minute. Could you not hear it?* He sat on the floor glaring up at her with narrowed eyes.

Eva looked at her workstation, surprised not to see her phone where she usually put it to alert her to the end of the sewing session.

Hrmph, he huffed. *Don't you believe me?* He asked when she didn't answer him, and he saw what she was doing.

"Sorry, Reuben, I was in the zone."

Yes, but more like the danger zone if you don't turn that blasted thing off, he said and stomped, if cats can do such a thing, back to his cushion in the bay window of the living room.

Eva clapped her hands together to get everyone's attention.

"Time to wrap it up for our show and tell but first I have to go get my phone to turn off the alarm. I forgot to bring it in with me and it is disrupting Reuben's beauty sleep."

Everyone was putting away their sewing machines and gathering up their fabrics and supplies with the exception of their projects in progress when she returned.

"Okay, we can do that show and tell now. Annalise, why don't you start?"

"It's going really well. I watched the Sandy Fischer tutorial on my iPad while I was doing the cutting and am stitching it together now. It's amazing how quickly it goes together. I'll have it finished in plenty of time before the memorial celebration."

She held up the blocks she'd finished so far. It was a modern twist on stars and pinwheels in vibrant shades of blues, yellows, and orange.

"The four corners will be a solid white so I can do something interesting with free motion quilting in those and then a wide border to finish it off. I might try doing some ruler work, but I haven't made up my mind yet about that."

"I can't wait to see it finished. The colors you picked really pop," Jennifer complimented.

"How about you, Sarah?"

"Mine is going great, too. I used one of the patterns Evelyn suggested in her newsletter email. I picked it because you start by making strip sets that you then sew into a tube before cutting it at forty-five-degree angles to make your blocks. I'd never used that technique before but I'm loving how it creates squares when you put them together. I chose solids instead of patterns which makes it look even more geometrical."

"Do you have some that aren't sewn together yet so we can see how that happens?" Eva asked.

"Sure!" She pulled four pieces from one of her two stacks and turned them to the proper alignment. "And then when you sew these together, it makes the contrasting light center instead of the dark one," she said as she placed them next to the others.

"How hard was it working with the tubes?" Annalise asked.

"As long as they're the same size, it's a breeze. Ask me how I know what happens if they're not!"

All five of the others nodded their heads, acknowledging they'd all been there, done that.

"I'm doing one of the patterns Evelyn suggested, too," Paul said. "I forgot to mention earlier that we've had a lot of our customers take a sign-up sheet, Jennifer. In fact, you might want to check with Evelyn to see if she needs more."

"That's amazing! I'll give her a call tomorrow morning. Let's see the one you picked out, Paul."

"Stars are my favorite block to make, and I love patterns that make a secondary design when you put them together. I think Nicky is going to have fun quilting it because of all the negative space this one creates." He placed several blocks together to demonstrate.

"I found several different designs for the pattern I picked which is called Summer Memories. The name is what caught my attention first. I love how it makes little baskets of flowers. The fabric Evelyn helped me pick out is sewing up like a dream. The blue fabric reminded me of the color of Summer's eyes. I'm about halfway finished with my project and hoped to get the top completely pieced by the time we were done tonight but didn't quite make it."

"It's beautiful, Jennifer," Annalise said.

"I haven't started sewing mine together yet, but my pieces are all cut and ready to go. It took me longer than I expected to do the cutting tonight," Sharon said when it was her turn. "Because Summer was involved as a counselor for summer camp, that's the name of the pattern I picked. Each block is a little different and it may have been more ambitious than I have time for but now that I have all the pieces cut, it should go more quickly. Here's the picture of what it will look like."

"If you find you need help with it, just let me know," Annalise offered.

"Thank you! Knowing that I've got backup takes some of the pressure off."

"That leaves me. The pattern I picked is Summer School which I thought was fitting since I was a teacher and Summer wanted to become one. I'm making each of the fish a different color and using up some of my stash in the process so a win-win all the way around."

"That's going to be adorable, Eva," Sarah said when Eva held up several of her blocks for everyone to see.

"Kudos to everyone." Eva said after they had each shown off their quilts. "You're all doing a terrific job. I can't wait to see all the finished quilts displayed in the cafeteria during the memorial."

CHAPTER SEVENTEEN

It was Jennifer's day off and she was busy at her sewing machine when the doorbell rang. Boscoe had been lying on his dog bed which Jennifer had put in the room so he would have a place to stay while she was sewing. He lifted his head at the sound of the bell and let out a single bark. She wasn't expecting anyone, but it was even more of a shock when she saw Detectives Phil Roberts and Dennis Smith when she opened the door. They had been involved with the case for her Aunt Sadie's murder and Annalise Jordan's break-in and related murder case. The identity of the killers in those cases had been discovered and their cases were pending so she couldn't imagine why they would be coming to see her.

"What a nice surprise, detectives. Would you like to come in?"

"Thank you, Mrs. Ryder," Roberts replied, and he and Dennis Smith followed Jennifer as she led the way to her living room with Boscoe bringing up the rear. Once the humans were seated, he placed himself next to Jennifer's knee, letting these men know that he would defend her if needed.

"Can I get you something to drink?" she asked.

"No, thank you. We don't want to take much of your time," Dennis Smith said.

The detectives looked at each other. Jennifer could tell they were uncomfortable but waited for them to explain their presence.

"I'm sure you're wondering why we're here," Phil Roberts began.

"Yes, I am. Does this have anything to do with my Aunt Sadie's case?" Jennifer asked, as the thought came to her that something might have gone wrong and Sadie's murderer, Stephen Hill, was going to be released.

"No, no. Everything is fine with that. The trial date has been set and the evidence against him is strong. Having his confession and DNA made it a slam dunk. We're here for another reason," Roberts said, pausing as though deciding how to proceed. "This is about the Summer Williams case. We, umm…"

The sound of the grandfather clock ticking filled the room as he fell silent.

"We were hoping you and your friends might be able to help us," Dennis Smith picked up the thread of conversation when it seemed Phil Roberts didn't know how to continue.

Jennifer realized it must have taken a lot for them to approach her. They were tip-toeing around admitting it was because of the Cozy Quilts Club members using their paranormal skills that the cases against Stephen Hill and Michael Granger had been solved when the detectives had run out of leads. She decided to feign ignorance that this was why they had come to her.

"How do you think we would be able to help?"

Once again, they looked at each other, their discomfort painfully evident.

"Are you thinking we might be able to use our special skills to find more clues about the accident?" she asked, trying to be diplomatic.

"Yes," Phil Roberts said, letting out his breath and looking relieved that he wouldn't have to actually say they wanted a team of paranormal amateur sleuths assisting with their case.

"I see. Well, I don't know if there's anything we can do but I can ask my Club if they would be willing to try. With the other cases we've been a part of, we had a personal connection to the crime. Other than knowing Summer through my children, we aren't as close to her case."

"We read that you are part of the event that's being planned for Summer and that gave us the idea to approach you. We've had some leads about who might have been the hit-and-run driver, but they haven't panned out. You were able to help us before, so we talked it over and decided it couldn't hurt to at least ask for your help."

"Should I assume you are here in an unofficial capacity?"

"That's correct. I'm sure you know it's not something the department would want to be making any statements about to the public," Smith said.

"I understand. I'm sure we can be discreet. Using our skills isn't something we've made any public announcements about either and planned to keep it that way," Jennifer said. "Of course, I can't speak for the others, so I can't give you an answer until we've talked it over. My guess is that they'll be happy to do whatever they can, though. Let me get back to you. I'll get in touch with them and ask if they can meet tonight so we would have an answer for you within the next couple of days."

"That's all we can ask. And thank you," Roberts said, and they both rose to leave.

Boscoe jumped to his feet when Jennifer also stood and moved out of the way, but stayed nearby when she followed the men to the door. They each handed her their business cards, and she promised once again to get back to them soon.

"Well, what do you think about that, Boscoe? It seems like the detectives are ready to believe us," she said reaching down to give him a pat on the head.

He whimpered and then gave a short bark in response.

"Now, if only Eva was here. She could tell me what you said."

CHAPTER EIGHTEEN

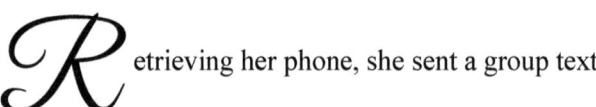

*R*etrieving her phone, she sent a group text.

> Can you all meet at my house tonight at 6:30? I'll explain when you get here but you're never going to believe what just happened!

She hit Send and waited to see if she got a response to her group text. Eva was the first to reply.

> You have my curiosity piqued. Count me in!

> Me, too!

Annalise added.

> I'll check with Ashley, but I don't think it will be a problem. Will let you know ASAP.

Sarah replied.

Jennifer had just settled in at her sewing machine when she heard the text notification from Sarah.

> I can be there. See you then!

The group gathered at Jennifer's eat-in kitchen table at six thirty as planned and although no one had asked, there was an undercurrent of excitement from each of them, wondering what could be the reason for the meeting.

Boscoe ping-ponged between each of the women, his tail wagging at full speed, allowing them to give him a pat on the head before dashing back to someone else. He finally settled long enough for Eva to speak with him.

"And how are you doing, Boscoe?" Eva asked, stroking his head and scratching behind his ears.

I'm doing much better. I still miss Sadie, but Jennifer's family is mine now and I'm happy to be here.

"Of course, you do. That's completely understandable, but I'm glad you're settling in here now. You have a good forever home." Eva told him and then repeated what he had said for the benefit of the others.

Jennifer smiled at Boscoe and took his face in her hands, scratching under his chin just the way he liked it.

"You'll always be one of the family, Boscoe."

He laid his chin on her leg, and she could tell from the adoring look in his eyes that he understood.

"So, what is this big news you have to talk to us about?" Annalise asked.

"I got a visit today from Detectives Smith and Roberts."

"You did?" Eva asked, and her eyebrows lifted.

"I did. They hadn't called first, so it came as a total surprise. At first, I was afraid they were going to tell me something went wrong, and Stephen Hill was going free but fortunately that wasn't why they showed up. It took a while to get them to finally tell me it was because they wanted to know if we could help them with the Summer Williams case."

The thought occurred to Jennifer that they could have all been looking into the same mirror. Their expressions were nearly identical as their jaws dropped and their eyes grew round as they sat in stunned silence.

Annalise was the first to speak. "Am I understanding correctly that they are asking for our *paranormal* help?"

"They didn't put it into those words, but that's exactly what they were asking," Jennifer said, a Cheshire cat smile on her face. "I asked them if they wanted us to use our 'special skills'" she said using air quotes, "and I wish I could have taken a picture of their faces when they realized they wouldn't have to actually say the words before they agreed that's what they were asking."

"I can't wait to tell Jim," Eva said, chuckling.

"If you do, just ask him to keep this on the QT," Jennifer said. "They also told me they're doing this unofficially. They admitted they're not getting anywhere with their investigation and have run out of leads. We helped them out before so they're willing to suspend disbelief in the woo woo if it means we can give them new information to go on."

"How do they think we can help?" Sarah asked.

"They didn't come right out with any specific requests, but I got the impression they're hoping we can figure that out. I told them I couldn't promise anything until we all had a chance to talk but that I would get back to them as soon as we'd made a decision. So, what do you all think?"

Annalise had been quiet but spoke up now. "I'm willing to at least try. Sarah might be the one who can help the most if she is able to communicate with Summer."

"I could go to the accident site in case Summer's presence is still there and try to connect with her," Sarah said. "If she hasn't passed over, that would be the most likely spot to find her."

"It doesn't seem likely you would find any evidence left on the scene that belonged to her but maybe something was missed. If not, I'll try to think of something else or a way to ask Debbie Williams if I could hold something that belonged to Summer. How I'd explain that could be tricky but if it somehow related to the memorial..." Jennifer's voice trailed off as she thought about how to accomplish that task.

"When I get home, I'll do a meditation to see if anything comes up for me," Annalise said when it appeared Jennifer wasn't about to continue.

Realizing her mind had wandered, Jennifer came back to the room. "It sounds like everyone is on board. Do I have your permission to contact the detectives to let them know we'll put our abilities to work and see what comes of it?"

"That's okay with me," Annalise said.

"Me, too," Sarah agreed.

"I don't know if there's any way I could help since there aren't any animals that we know of who would have seen the accident. I'll do what I can, though," Eva offered.

"It sounds like we're all on board. I'll let them know tomorrow that we're on the case."

CHAPTER NINETEEN

∼

The next day Annalise was returning from an errand in Bangor. Her route took her to the accident site, and she felt a nudge to stop. A small white wooden cross had been erected just outside the shoulder of the road with Summer's name and the date of the accident painted on it. Covering the ground around it and reaching halfway up the cross were bouquets of sunflowers, fading now.

Sunflowers must have been her favorite flower.

The sky was gray and a light rain was falling adding to the melancholy of the scene. Someone had placed a teddy bear on the ground in front of the flowers and the rain was matting its fur. A pair of running shoes had been hung by its laces over the cross's horizontal beam. The shoes had a disquieting effect on Annalise. Instead of being a solace, it sent shivers up her spine. She pulled her car onto the shoulder of the road facing the memorial and put her hazard lights on to make sure any cars approaching from behind would see that she was pulled over. She closed her eyes, slowed her breathing, and slipped into that state between sleep and wakefulness when most of her visions came to her. At first, she wasn't having any response but then as though she was watching a movie through the driver's point of view, the scene played out exactly as the accident happened that day. She even felt the chilly air coming from the air conditioner on her face and heard the music playing on the radio.

Once the scene had progressed to the point at which the car was driving away without the driver having gotten out, Annalise returned to full awareness of her surroundings. She retrieved her phone and pressed Sarah's number.

"She didn't know she hit anyone."

CHAPTER TWENTY

~

Sarah and Ashley were enjoying a rare lazy day together. The rain had given them an excuse to put off their outdoor chores and stay inside snuggled up on the couch. Ashley was at one end reading and Sarah was at the other with their Golden Retriever, Max, stretched out between them. The music playing softly in the background was interrupted by the ringtone of Sarah's phone. Ashley looked up from her book, a slight scowl on her face as Sarah picked up the phone. Her knee-jerk reaction based on previous occasions was that it was Sarah's work interrupting their day off. Expecting it to be about work, too, Sarah shrugged her shoulders as a silent response of *I don't have a choice* before seeing Annalise's name on the screen.

"Annalise?"

Annalise heard the question in Sarah's voice and realized she hadn't even said hello.

"Yes, it's me. Sorry. I just had a vision and I guess I was still in the moment. I'm here at the accident site and I could see the accident happening from the driver's point of view."

"Ah, that's what you meant. The driver didn't realize she had hit Summer. How can that be?"

"It was a case of a distracted driver. She had taken her eyes off the road to try to reach her phone. It was in her purse on the passenger seat when it rang. She was struggling to get it out and the purse fell onto the floor with the phone still in it and she bent over to try to pick it up. I couldn't see Summer in my vision even before the driver bent over, but the car was close to the curve at that point. I think she must have bent over just as Summer came around the curve and didn't even realize she was there. The impression I got was that the car drifted over to the shoulder because she jerked the steering wheel when she felt the impact. After the accident, she stopped and looked in her mirror, but nothing was on the road, so she drove off."

"Could you see the driver's face when she looked in the mirror?"

"No, the angle wasn't right. I was only able to tell it was a woman from what I saw of her hand," Annalise said with disappointment.

"I could probably go there later today if the rain lets up. Will you be home? I can stop at your house after I'm done."

"Yes, I'll be home. I'd love to have you stop and tell me if you were able to make contact."

"I'll see you later then."

Sarah disconnected the call and saw that Ashley was looking at her inquisitively, her book now resting in her lap.

"Was that about the hit and run case?" Ashley asked.

"Yeah, I thought I might be able to connect with the girl who was killed. I hadn't planned to go today but Annalise just stopped at the accident site and had a vision. Would you mind if I gave it a try later on? I don't think it would take long."

Ashley sighed. "Sure, go ahead. At least it isn't work. And I expect a full report when you get home."

~

Sarah arrived later that afternoon and parked in the same spot Annalise had used earlier. The rain had stopped and the clouds that had filled the sky earlier were giving way to patches of blue. She remained sitting in the car, closed her eyes and focused inward to block out all external noises. The sounds of crows squawking overhead and cars passing by made it difficult but at last she was able to achieve the meditative state necessary when she was the one to make contact. When the spirit of someone who had already passed wanted to initiate a conversation this wasn't necessary. They had no difficulty connecting, but their sense of timing had created some awkward moments for Sarah over the years. Several minutes passed without success. Sarah opened her eyes but wasn't ready to give up yet. If she could find the spot where Summer's body had come to rest, her odds might improve. She thought about putting on her hazard lights but decided against it, not wanting to bring more attention to herself and be interrupted if she was able to contact Summer. It was more likely another car would drive by if they saw the car was empty, assuming it had broken down. She checked to make sure no one was coming and got out of the car. Walking to the shoulder, she looked down the slope trying to imagine where Summer had been found. She wasn't seeing any obvious sign of the location but felt a nudge to walk to where the grass was thicker. Carefully side stepping down the embankment now slick from the rain, she made her way to the spot and walked slowly in a circle waiting for any indication Summer was still there and wanted to make contact. This was what Sarah thought of as her internal guidance system version of you're getting warmer. She was about to give up when a soft voice sounded in her head.

Why are you here?

"My name is Sarah. I've come to talk to you about the day you died, Summer. Would you be okay with that?"

I guess.

Sarah kneeled down on her heels to conceal her presence from passersby trying to avoid as much of the wet grass as possible. "Thank you. I know this must be difficult. Do you remember what happened that day?"

I was out for a run. It was so hot that day. I was thinking I should have gone earlier when it was cooler, but I didn't want to miss a day. I was going to do the Boston Marathon next year and I had to be in shape.

"Yes, someone told me you were planning to do that. Do you remember seeing the car coming toward you?"

Yes. I had just come around the corner. I wasn't worried at first but then the car started drifting toward the shoulder and when I looked at the windshield, I couldn't see a driver. My brain wasn't making sense of that, and I waited too long to jump. I should have jumped sooner.

Sarah's heart broke hearing the sadness in Summer's voice.

How could there be no driver?

This time Sarah could hear the confusion Summer had experienced that day.

"A friend told me the driver was distracted and had bent over to pick up her phone that had fallen off the passenger seat. She didn't see you. Are you saying that you didn't see the driver at all before the car hit you?"

No. It was like the car was driving itself. I never saw anyone.

Sarah's hopes fell. They were not going to be any further ahead than before about having a description of the driver.

Are my parents and my sister okay? I don't want them to be sad.

Once again, the strings of Sarah's heart tugged.

"I don't know them but I think it's okay if they're sad. They need to grieve for you. They have a lot of people in the community helping them, though. And everyone wants to find the driver who did this to you."

I'm sorry I couldn't tell you who it was.

"That's okay, Summer. We'll keep trying. Are you ready to pass over to the other side now? I can help you if that's what you want."

I'm not ready yet. I don't know why but I think I need to stay just a little longer.

"I understand. I'll come back again and if you change your mind, I can help you then if you need it."

Thank you. Would you tell my family I love them?

"I don't know if I can do that, Summer," Sarah said. "They don't know me, and they might think I was playing a cruel trick on them if I told them I had been in contact with you."

I suppose you're right. I hadn't thought of that.

"I don't think you need to worry, though. I'm sure they know how much you loved them." She hesitated, debating whether she should continue but the sadness in Summer's voice caused her to be impulsive. "If there's any way I can tell them without upsetting them, I will," she said, her voice catching. "I promise." She hoped that was a promise she wouldn't have to break.

Sarah walked back up the hill and sat for a moment in her car to settle herself before starting the engine and driving on to Annalise's house.

CHAPTER TWENTY-ONE

~

*J*ennifer put away the vacuum cleaner and dusting supplies after finishing her usual Saturday house cleaning chores. She looked at the clock and was dismayed to find it had taken longer than expected. Knowing she'd have to hurry to get ready for the memorial committee meeting wasn't helping relieve her annoyance.

I don't know why we have to do this on a Saturday. Or at least just do a zoom meeting so we don't have to take even more time to drive there and back.

She collected her committee folder and walked to the back of the house to let David know she was leaving. The drizzle of rain that morning had given way to partly sunny skies. He was astride his beloved John Deere riding mower at the far end of the lawn with his back to her. Even if he had been facing her, between the roar of the motor and the protective ear gear he had on under his baseball cap, he wouldn't have heard her. Why he was even mowing wet grass was beyond her. The only thing she could think of was that he was trying to get in as much lawn time as possible before the mower would have to be put away for the winter. She shook her head as she watched, befuddled about his love of lawn care. He'd told her once it was his Zen time. There was something about the rhythm of riding back and forth and seeing the rows of grass take shape that put him into a meditative state. When he turned back toward the house and was about fifty feet away, she raised a hand over her head and began waving it in big arcs hoping to catch his attention so he would stop. At first, he didn't notice and her annoyance went up another notch on the scale. Finally, as he was about to turn the mower around and begin the next row, he looked up and seeing her now frantic waving, he cut the engine.

"What's up?" he asked with a confused look.

His calm tone and apparent obliviousness to her urgent signals to stop cranked up her annoyance to eleven.

"I'm leaving now to go to the memorial committee meeting."

His head cocked at an angle, and she knew he was trying to put her statement into context.

"It's the special meeting. I put it on the whiteboard." She didn't even try to hide her irritation.

"Ohhh, right. Now I remember." He nodded his head and smiled before turning the engine back on and gave her a wave. "I'll see you when you get back." He turned the mower around and drove off leaving her speechless.

She stomped back toward the garage fuming. She tossed her purse and folder onto the passenger seat and backed the car out onto the driveway. She'd driven a half mile down the road before she realized it wasn't David she was angry with. It was Rebecca for calling the extra meeting. Jennifer couldn't imagine what it was about. At their last meeting everyone was on top of their assignments and things were running smoothly. What could possibly have happened since then that couldn't wait until their next regular meeting? Her quilt for the Linus Project still wasn't done and she'd planned to finish it over the weekend. This was setting her back even more.

From the looks on the faces and body language of several other members of the committee, she wasn't the only one who didn't want to be here. A few were still milling about at the back of the room, coffee cups in hand, when Rebecca entered the room. She didn't say anything but her glare in their direction brought them to their seats. Her face was pale and there were dark circles under her eyes. Unlike her usually put together appearance, today her clothes were rumpled as though she'd pulled them out of her hamper. Granted it was a Saturday, but this went far beyond the definition of weekend casual and the contrast was striking.

She looks terrible. It looks like she's lost some weight, too.

"Can I have your attention, please. We're on a tight deadline here, folks, so we need to stop the chatter and get down to business."

The room quieted but the negative energy Rebecca was projecting was doing nothing to improve everyone's mood. Instead of her usual friendly disposition, Rebecca was all business today. Jennifer glanced around to see if she was the only one who noticed but it was obvious Rebecca's vibe was making everyone uncomfortable.

"Somebody got up on the wrong side of the bed," Jennifer heard Brad Towne mutter under his breath from the seat behind her. She lowered her head and put her hand over her mouth to hide her smile.

"Mike, why don't you start with your committee report and then we'll go around the room for the others. What progress have you made since we last met?"

He opened the file he had on his desk and gave his report.

"Justine, you're next," Rebecca said, her tone brusque. She didn't even thank Mike for his report before moving on.

Jennifer sneaked a look at Marianne who was sitting beside

her in the next row and they both raised their eyebrows. This was not the same Rebecca McCormick who had been steering the committee since they first met.

"Jennifer, what progress have you made with the publicity and the quilt project?"

What's gotten into her? Jennifer thought. *I should make sure she's okay once the meeting is over. This isn't like her at all.*

"Jennifer."

The sharp tone in Rebecca's voice snapped Jennifer's attention back to the room.

"Oh, um…. it's going well. The article in The Bangor News got the word out to the broader community. We've put posters in the downtown shops, and I've been coordinating with Quilting Essentials for the quilt donations. They've given out fifty sign-up sheets already and have asked me to bring more. I don't think everyone who took a form will come through with a quilt but if even a quarter of them do, we'll have a beautiful display for the cafeteria. I might need some help hanging them since we won't be able to start until the morning of the service. If anyone could volunteer to help, we would be most appreciative."

Several hands went up and Jennifer jotted down their names.

"What about the TV interview? I'm still waiting for you to tell me when you can be available."

The irritation in Rebecca's voice was unmistakable. Jennifer could see people fidgeting in their seats in her periphery. She wasn't the only one Rebecca had made uncomfortable. Some of the anger she'd felt earlier started to rise but this wasn't the time or place to call Rebecca out. *Pick your battles.* She swallowed to keep her temper from slipping out.

"I'm sorry, I was waiting for you to confirm with me. I'd left a message with Gretchen Fields on Wednesday and assumed she had forwarded it to you."

"You should have sent the message directly to me. We've

wasted two days and the reporter for Channel 6 told me they might have to drop the story if I don't get back to her by Monday."

"I'm sorry, I thought..." Jennifer began but was cut off by Rebecca.

"Never mind, I'll get in touch with them today and if they're still willing to do the story, I'll let you know. Trudy?" she said turning to Trudy Mills making it clear she had dismissed Jennifer.

Jennifer's cheeks turned red, and she felt like she was back in high school being reprimanded for not turning in her homework on time. That hadn't ever happened to her, but she'd seen it with enough other students to recognize the rebuke. Marianne took her hand and gave it a squeeze before quickly pulling it away in case Rebecca was looking in their direction. The action had been fleet, but it made Jennifer feel better. Today when the meeting broke up there was an exodus for the door. The only thing that passed for conversation as everyone rushed out was the exchange of raised eyebrows.

Jennifer hung back as the others left, determined to speak to Rebecca. There was something going on and even though Rebecca's words had stung, Jennifer's empathetic nature made her want to make sure she was okay. When they were finally alone, Jennifer walked up to her desk where Rebecca was gathering up her notes.

"Becky, is everything alright?"

Rebecca jumped, dropping the notes she had in her hand onto the desk.

"I thought everyone was gone." The smell of alcohol rolled off the woman.

"I didn't mean to startle you. What's wrong, Becky? You're not yourself today," she said and put her hand on Rebecca's shoulder. Without warning, Jennifer's mind was filled with the sensation of being behind the wheel of a car and she immediately recognized the corner of the road where Summer had been hit. Just as it had for Annalise, she saw and felt the sensations through the point of view of the driver as the accident happened.

A wave of nausea came over Jennifer and she swallowed hard as she removed her hand from Rebecca's shoulder. It felt like minutes had passed but it had only been seconds. She blinked and willed herself to remain calm. Rebecca had been looking down at the desk and by the time she looked up, Jennifer had regained her composure. She didn't want to let on that she'd tapped into what Rebecca had been thinking in that instant of contact.

"I'm fine. Just a little tired and I want the memorial to be perfect. Summer deserves the best celebration we can give."

"Of course. If it's becoming too much, I hope you know we'll all step up to give you a hand."

"Thanks." Rebecca paused and for a moment Jennifer thought she was going to open up, but instead she looked down at her papers. "I appreciate it, but I'll be fine."

She didn't look fine, but Jennifer realized she wasn't ready to confront Rebecca. "Okay, sure. Well, give me a call if you need anything or if you just want to talk."

Jennifer sat in her car thinking about the meeting and Rebecca. Something was not right. She needed to talk this through but not with David. She sent a group text to Annalise and the others instead.

> Just got out of a memorial committee meeting. Something weird is going on. Need to talk.

Her phone pinged immediately.

> We need to talk to you, too!!! We're all at my house. Get here quick!!

This day was heading in a direction Jennifer hadn't expected.

She wondered what it was the ladies had to tell her. Only one way to find out. She put the car in drive.

CHAPTER TWENTY-TWO

∽

Sarah's and Eva's cars were in Annalise's driveway when Jennifer arrived. All the way there she had been trying to think of a plan for how to deal with the information she'd received when she had touched Rebecca. Nothing had come to her but once she shared it with the others, they might have suggestions.

Annalise led her into the living room where Sarah and Eva were sitting. Just seeing the others helped put her at ease. In the short time they'd come together as a group, they had formed a relationship that she had no doubt would last. They truly were friends forever. She declined Annalise's offer of a beverage and sat in one of the comfy chairs and Annalise sat in the other opposite from Eva and Sarah.

"Why don't you start, Sarah?" Eva suggested. "We've been waiting for you to get here so we would all be in on what's happened at the same time," she said to Jennifer.

Jennifer nodded and turned her attention to Sarah.

"I went to the accident site and down the embankment to

where I thought Summer might have been found. At first, I wasn't sure if she was still there but then she spoke. She said she never saw the driver because it looked like no one was driving the car. She was trying to figure out what was happening, and it was too late for her to get out of the way by the time she realized the car was going to hit her. She's so sad and is worried about her family. She wanted to know if they are okay and asked me to tell them she loves them. That nearly broke me, and it makes me want to cry even now. I promised her I would let them know. I plan to keep that promise but now I have to figure out how I'm going to do that. I told her we were doing our best to find the driver."

"Let me think about that. I'm not sure how Debbie or Ralph would respond but if I can come up with something, I'll share that with you," Jennifer said.

Annalise picked up the conversation then. "I hadn't planned to stop but when I was coming back from an errand today and saw the cross and all the mementos people have left at the roadside memorial, I felt compelled to stop. This happened before Sarah got there. I focused on quieting my mind and then I had a vision that I'm sure was from the driver's point of view. I could tell it was a female driving because I could see her hand reaching down to try to get her phone out of her purse and then it fell onto the floor on the passenger side. I felt the impact when the car hit Summer and heard the sound it made. The driver was bent over and didn't even realize Summer had been on the side of the road. By the time she stopped the car and looked in the mirror, Summer was already hidden in the weeds, so she had no idea it was a person. The impression I received was that she thought she had hit an animal that had run back off the road and that's why she drove off."

Jennifer nodded her head when Annalise was finished. It matched what she had seen when she touched Rebecca.

"That's exactly what I saw, too. But I know who it is."

CHAPTER TWENTY-THREE

~

Surprise and excitement registered on everyone's faces.
"How do you know?" Eva asked.
Jennifer recounted what happened at the committee meeting.
"I had the exact same vision that you did, Annalise. She's the driver. I know it without question. She must have been thinking about it when I touched her."
Everyone was quiet as they processed that bit of information.
"It struck me that something was off the other day when I was in the principal's office to drop off more sign-up forms and the tote to collect the quilts. Gretchen Fields, the principal's secretary, asked if we had heard any more about the driver. I thought I saw something in Rebecca's expression like she knew something, but it passed so quickly I thought I must have imagined it. Or maybe I just didn't want to believe that it could be true. Now that I know what I do, I must have been right after all. She looked scared, and hurried off right after we said we hadn't heard any news about the driver. I suspect she didn't want to be around if the conversation continued."

"Do you think this is enough to pass on to Detectives Smith and Roberts?" Eva asked.

"Absolutely!" Annalise said. "This is just the sort of information they were hoping we would discover. It isn't enough for them to make an arrest, but they can dig deeper now that they know who to focus on."

"I agree," Jennifer said. "I'll call them right now while we're all together. They both put their cell phone numbers on their cards so I should be able to reach them."

She picked up her purse and found their cards tucked into her wallet. Pulling out her cell phone, she dialed the number for Dennis Smith who answered on the second ring.

"Detective Smith, this is Jennifer Ryder. I'm here with the other ladies from the Cozy Quilts Club. Would you and Detective Roberts be able to meet us at Annalise Jordan's house? We have information we need to tell you. We know who was driving the car that killed Summer Williams."

CHAPTER TWENTY-FOUR

The detectives arrived within half an hour. They were dressed in jeans and button-down shirts rather than their usual suits.

They must be off duty.

Annalise already knew from the way they had handled her situation they were dedicated and went the extra mile to solve cases. Seeing they were willing to put in time while off-duty gave them extra brownie points in her assessment.

She brought them into the living room where the others were still seated. Their greeting of each of the women wasn't unfriendly, but they stood with their shoulders slightly hunched. As they extended a hand in greeting, they ducked their heads as if nervous to meet their gazes. Their body language practically screamed their embarrassment to be there despite the fact they were the ones who had asked for help.

"Thank you for calling us Mrs. Ryder. First, who is the driver?" Detective Smith asked.

"We have reason to believe it's Rebecca McCormick, the

teacher at Summer's high school who is coordinating the memorial service in her honor."

Phil Roberts had brought a notebook and pen with him and began taking notes. "What led you to believe she's the one responsible?" His tone was even and business-like but Jennifer didn't sense he was patronizing her.

"Today two of us had a vision separately of the accident happening from the driver's point of view and Sarah... Well, I'll let Annalise and Sarah tell how it happened for them and then I'll jump in."

Annalise looked to Sarah who nodded for her to begin.

"I was driving by the accident scene and was compelled to pull over. As you know, I'm a psychic and sometimes I get information from various points of view." She recounted her vision for them as she had for the Quilt Club. "My impression is that she honestly didn't realize she'd hit Summer at the time. It wasn't apparent to me if she made the connection later as I was only seeing the accident as it happened there."

Sarah picked up the account. "You've probably figured out that I'm the person who can speak to dead people. I was at the accident scene after Annalise had been there and was able to make contact with Summer. Unfortunately, she wasn't able to see the driver to be able to give me a description or name but what she said corroborated what Annalise had seen in her vision. When the car was coming at Summer, she said it looked like there was no driver. She was so surprised she was momentarily frozen there and took too long to jump out of the way. She told me more, but it wasn't related to identifying the driver."

Jennifer continued their accounts.

"We had a meeting earlier today of the memorial service committee. Rebecca McCormick was acting out of character..."

"In what way?" Dennis Smith interrupted.

"She was very brusque. Usually, she is a pleasant person to be with and even though she's business-like, it's done in a way that comes across as friendly. That was not how she was today. I stayed after the meeting to see if something was wrong and perhaps, I could help. When I was closer to her, I could smell alcohol on her breath. Do you remember that my ability is psychometry? That's when someone gets information by touching a person or an object of theirs."

The detectives nodded to indicate they did.

"When I put my hand on her shoulder, I also had a vision of the accident happening from her point of view. At that time, I didn't know about Annalise's vision, so it wasn't as though that was already in my consciousness. I knew… know… without any doubt in my mind that Rebecca McCormick is the one who killed Summer."

"I assume you didn't tell Ms. McCormick about your vision?" Dennis asked.

"No, and I don't think she suspected anything was wrong. She wasn't looking at my face when that was happening, and I was able to compose myself before she did look up. I thought I should wait to speak with both of you first."

"Do you know what kind of car she drives?" Roberts asked.

"Yes, it's a silver sedan with four doors. It's either a Toyota or a Nissan. I'm not sure which but you should be able to check that out."

Dennis looked toward Phil to make sure he wrote that down in his notes.

"Have you seen her car since the accident? Does it have any damage to the right front side?" he asked.

"Now that you mention it, we were leaving the parking lot at the same time after the meeting before this and I don't remember any damage," Jennifer said, discouraged now thinking she might have been wrong about Rebecca.

Detective Roberts saw her reaction so stepped in to reassure her.

"That may be a good thing. Assuming it was her, it means

she's had the car repaired. We can start calling repair shops to ask if they've recently done work on a car with her license plate. We can also check her credit cards to see if there is a charge for the repairs. It's possible she paid cash, but the repair shop should still have a record of the transaction."

"Unless they're skimming for any cash deals," Eva suggested.

"That's possible, but they still would have had to buy parts and since we're not the IRS, they may be more willing to admit they did the repairs knowing the situation and that we're not planning to audit their books." Dennis said.

"Do you want me to see if Rebecca would confess if I confronted her?" Jennifer asked.

Both detectives sat quietly, thinking over the pros and cons.

Phil Roberts was the first to speak. "Don't make an issue of it yet. I think we'd like a chance to check with the body shops in the area first. Let's hold that as a Plan B. You're absolutely sure it was her?"

"There's not a doubt in my mind."

CHAPTER TWENTY-FIVE

~

Jennifer was at work on Monday when she got a call from Rebecca. Her stomach clenched when she saw Rebecca's name on her cell phone screen, but she answered hoping her tone came across like any other time they'd spoken.

"Jennifer, it's Becky McCormick. First, I want to apologize for my rude behavior on Saturday. I've been feeling overwhelmed lately and was out-of-sorts with everyone during the meeting. I plan to apologize to the others at our next meeting, but since I have you now, I didn't want to wait."

"Of course, thank you for saying so. I admit I was surprised as you're not usually like that. It's why I stayed behind to see if I could help."

"I'm glad you did. It made me realize how inappropriate I had been. But that's not the only reason I'm calling. Channel 6 would still like to do the interview and wondered if tomorrow afternoon at three thirty would work?"

Jennifer checked her calendar to make sure she hadn't

forgotten another appointment before replying she could be there.

"That's wonderful. You've been doing a terrific job of getting the word out, but this should reach even more people than you've been able to."

"I agree and anything I can do to make this a success, I'm happy to help."

"Why don't you come to my classroom around three o'clock and we can chat with the reporter before they begin the actual interview?"

"I can do that. I'll see you then," Jennifer said and disconnected the call.

She was wrapped in her thoughts wondering how she was going to be able to act normally around Becky now that she was aware of what she'd done. David came out of his office, coffee mug in hand. He'd been on his way to the coffee station for a refill but stopped midway when he noticed Jennifer.

"Penny for your thoughts," David said.

"I'm sorry, what?"

"I said penny for your thoughts. You look like you're a million miles away."

Jennifer hadn't told David yet about the vision she'd seen with Rebecca and debated whether she should until they had more conclusive evidence, but trusted he wouldn't share it with anyone else. Detectives Smith and Roberts had impressed upon the Club members that they wanted to keep their meeting under wraps as long as possible to give them time to check for repairs made to Rebecca's car.

"What I'm about to tell you has to be kept between you and me," she said.

"This sounds serious," he said, his brows furrowed. He took the seat in front of Jennifer's desk giving her his full attention.

"I learned something at the last committee meeting that I have to keep secret for now, but I know I can trust you. It's been weighing on me and I think sharing it with you will help. The ladies in the quilt group know but I don't like keeping things from you."

"You know I won't tell a soul if you say I shouldn't and if it will bring you some peace of mind to share, please do."

"I need to back things up before I tell you what happened at the meeting. Last week Detectives Smith and Roberts came to see me."

David's eyebrows raised. "The detectives who worked on your Aunt Sadie's case?"

"Yes. They're the same ones who were involved with Annalise's incident. I think they finally believe that we have paranormal abilities. They looked embarrassed but perhaps desperation overruled, and they came to me to see if we would try to break something open on Summer's case. They knew I was part of the memorial from the article in The Bangor News which is why they came to me. We hadn't planned to be actively finding clues to solve it but after the detectives asked, we did. Sarah made contact with Summer but learned that she hadn't seen the driver. Annalise saw it happening from the driver's point of view but never saw her face. Circling back to what I started to say earlier, you're not going to believe this, but I've learned that Rebecca McCormick was the driver."

CHAPTER TWENTY-SIX

This time David's silence was from shock.

"You're sure?" he finally asked Jennifer.

"Yes. I had one of my psychometry visions when I put my hand on her shoulder at the last meeting. She must have been thinking about it when I did because it came through as though I was looking through her eyes as it happened."

"Have you told the detectives?"

"Yes, we asked them to come to Annalise's and we each told them what we'd experienced. They're looking into Rebecca now. Her car doesn't have any damage but they're going on the theory that she had it repaired quickly so no one would suspect. She drives a silver sedan which would have been a red flag if anyone had seen it with damage on the right side."

"What did Rebecca do when that happened?"

"She didn't see my face and I was able to hide my surprise in time. She was the one who just called. We're doing an interview tomorrow at the high school for Channel 6. I just hope I'll be able to keep up the charade while I'm around her."

"I understand why you would be worried, but I think you'll do okay. It might even be that a part of her would be relieved to have it out in the open even though the consequences won't be easy. If you do slip up, it might be the impetus she needs to come forward to confess."

"Maybe. When I got closer to her, I smelled alcohol, and it was only mid-day. I think she might be drinking to deal with what happened."

"I can't imagine what it would be like knowing you've taken someone else's life. But add in leaving the scene and then pretending to be concerned by heading up the memorial service is either someone whose guilt is crushing them or on the opposite end of the spectrum, the behavior of a sociopath. I don't see Rebecca being a sociopath."

"I agree. I just hope she decides to confess and take her chances with the justice system before she has a breakdown."

CHAPTER TWENTY-SEVEN

When Jennifer arrived the next day right at three as Rebecca had requested, the news crew was already setting up their equipment.

"Did I misunderstand about what time I should come?" she asked.

"No, you're fine. The crew arrived a little early so they can begin getting the camera and lighting arranged," Rebecca said, a smile on her face.

This was the Rebecca Jennifer was used to seeing. She wondered if it was an act for the benefit of the reporter and crew or if it had been the alcohol that affected her mood when they'd last seen each other.

The reporter, a young woman in her early thirties with long brown hair and a trim figure, extended her hand for Jennifer to shake. "I'm Melanie Adams from Channel 6. You must be Jennifer Ryder."

"Yes, I'm Jennifer. It's nice to meet you, Melanie. I've seen you on the six PM edition."

"While we're waiting for the crew to finish, I thought we could do a practice interview to help you be more comfortable once the camera starts rolling. It helps if you forget about them as much as possible and pretend it's just us having a conversation," she said giving them a big smile.

"We'll do our best, won't we, Jennifer?" Rebecca said cheerily.

Too cheerily, Jennifer thought. This is all an act she's putting on so no one will catch on that there's more going on under the surface.

"I'll at least try," she said, using the same cheery tone Rebecca had.

The reporter gave them more instructions about looking at her instead of the camera and then asked them questions about the memorial service. By the time the actual interview began, Jennifer was much more comfortable and had forgotten about the camera rolling in the background and it was over in no time.

"Unless we have a breaking news story that will bump this, we should be able to air it tonight. It won't be edited in time for the six o'clock time slot, but it's plenty of time for the eleven o'clock edition. We'll repeat it for the next two or three broadcasts, so you'll get a lot of exposure for the event," Melanie informed them.

"Thank you again for doing this. It means so much to all of us to honor Summer's memory. The entire school has been affected by her absence. I'm hoping it will bring some comfort to her family, too. It must be incredibly difficult for them," Rebecca was saying.

Jennifer kept her face impassive but inside she could feel her anger rising. Rebecca was putting on a good show for Melanie and everyone else. Knowing she was the one responsible and not being able to say anything wasn't going to be easy. She hoped the detectives were able to get the information they needed so they could arrest her soon because she wasn't sure how much longer she could remain silent. Her thoughts had drifted but she was brought back to the moment when Melanie caught her attention to say good-bye.

"Thank you, Ms. McCormick. You're to be commended for putting together this event. I hope it all goes well. I can't imagine it not being a success with you in charge."

"You're too kind. I've had a lot of help. When Principal Jackson first raised the idea at a teacher staff meeting, I knew I had to be the one to volunteer."

"Well, it looks like the crew has everything packed, so we'll be going."

Rebecca turned to Jennifer once they had left the room and smiled. "I think that went very well, don't you?"

Her last comment about being the one to volunteer had tipped the scales and Jennifer realized she couldn't stay quiet any longer.

"Becky, I know you were the one…"

CHAPTER TWENTY-EIGHT

*B*efore she could finish the sentence, Nicole came into the room.

"There you are, Mom. I'm so glad I caught you before you left. Matt has to stay for soccer practice, and I missed the bus."

Becky was giving Jennifer a wary look but didn't ask her to finish her thought, making Jennifer think she might have known what she was about to say.

"Sure, honey. I was just about to leave. I'll see you soon, Ms. McCormick," she said remembering to use her surname for Nicole's benefit.

"Right! Wednesday night at the next committee meeting," Rebecca said, her voice casual, and she was smiling but her eyes didn't reflect it.

She tried to concentrate on Nicole's conversation during the ride home, but Jennifer's thoughts kept going back to Rebecca and she chastised herself for nearly blurting out her accusation that Rebecca was the driver. *I blew it! She knows I know something.* She would have to call the detectives and confess what she'd done, or almost done, and ask how they wanted her to proceed. As soon as they got home, she went to her bedroom so she would have privacy and called Phil Roberts whose business card was the first one she pulled out of her wallet.

"Detective Roberts," he said after picking up on the second ring.

"Hi, this is Jennifer Ryder. I may have made a huge mistake."

There was a brief pause before he replied. "Can you elaborate on that?"

"I was with Rebecca McCormick this afternoon doing an interview for Channel 6 and I'm very sorry, but her comments about how much she wanted to help and honor Summer's memory struck a nerve with me. After the TV crew left, I was just about to tell her I knew she was the driver, but my daughter came in the room before I got to the part where I was going to accuse her. I could see from her expression that she suspects I know the truth. Have I totally blown this for you?"

He was quiet and Jennifer held her breath waiting for the reprimand.

"I don't think so, Mrs. Ryder," he said at last. "We still haven't found the repair shop that fixed her car but we're expanding our search to independent shops and in neighboring towns. It may cause her to slip up if she thinks you know something. She may be thinking she's gotten away with it and there's no way anyone could tie her to the accident. From what you said about the alcohol on her breath, though, her conscience could be kicking in. There's no need to force the issue. I think just having her aware that she's under suspicion will put her off balance. That's when people make mistakes."

The tension in Jennifer's body relaxed.

"It's such a relief to hear you say that. Ever since it happened, I've been worried that it would have the opposite effect and make her even more likely to deny her involvement."

"I won't lie that it isn't a possibility, but she's not a career criminal and sooner or later the guilt of what she did will be too much."

"So, if I have another opportunity to approach her about this, should I go ahead?"

"Let's just say I won't tell you don't do it if the opportunity comes up, but you'll have to be the judge of when the appropriate time will be."

"Thank you for the advice, Detective Roberts. I'll let you know if I do and what her reaction is."

"You're most welcome. And, please, call me Phil. I think we've gotten past the formalities."

"I think you're right," she said chuckling. "Please call me Jennifer."

ON THE PREVIOUS times Jennifer had arrived at a committee meeting, many of the volunteers had gathered in small groups either at the desks or standing at the back of the room engaged in conversation and occasional laughter. They all knew their reason for being there was serious, but some levity didn't affect their ability to perform their tasks. As she glanced around the room, hardly anyone was talking and the few who were, did so in hushed tones.

It feels like Rebecca sucked the life out of us.

Jennifer smiled at Marianne as she took her usual seat beside her. Before she had a chance to say hello, Rebecca bustled into the room and deposited her tote bag on her desk. She walked back to stand in front of the room, her arms hanging in front of her with her hands clasped, and her head was bowed as though she was collecting her thoughts. She took a deep breath before looking up at the people gathered there. All eyes were on Rebecca, and you could have heard the proverbial pin drop.

"Before we get started, I want to say how sorry I am for my

behavior at our last meeting. I was very short with everyone. No, that's not quite true. I was *rude* with everyone, and I was taking out some of my personal problems on you. It was unprofessional and none of you deserved to be treated that way. I want you to know how much I have appreciated your help and the time that you've volunteered to make this event a success. I hope you can forgive me. I won't let it happen again."

Jennifer shifted uncomfortably in her seat as she thought about the "personal problems" Rebecca was having. She observed several others doing the same, although for very different reasons.

"Of course," a few people replied. Whether their sentiments were authentic or spoken merely out of politeness, Jennifer wasn't sure.

"Thank you. Before we get started with the subcommittee reports, I'd like to update you about the interview Jennifer and I did for Channel 6. Jennifer handled it like a pro, and it was a real comfort to have her with me so I wouldn't get a case of stage fright. The broadcast was delayed due to other stories taking priority, but Melanie Adams let me know that it should be on tonight's late-night report and repeated throughout the day tomorrow. Don't forget to set your DVRs!"

The rest of the meeting proceeded without incident and the tension that had been in the room when they first arrived had abated. Jennifer kept watching for signs from Rebecca that anything was amiss between them but if there was, she was doing a much better job of hiding it.

Since her conversation with Phil Roberts, she had debated internally about approaching Rebecca. She considered letting it go but she was positive her vision hadn't been wrong, and she had Phil's blessing to approach Rebecca. Her decision made, she hung back until the room had emptied and then walked to the desk where Rebecca was sitting.

"Do you know what psychometry is?" she asked.

Rebecca blinked in surprise. "I believe it's supposed to be a way for a person to get information from an object when they touch it. That's a rather off-the-wall question. Why are you asking me about it?"

"I haven't made a big deal about letting people know I have that gift for a number of reasons, which I'm sure you can figure out without my going into them," she said, keeping eye contact with Rebecca.

"Why are you telling me this now?"

"It's not something that happens all the time. When I put my hand on your shoulder after the last meeting and asked if you were alright, it did. I could see what you were thinking about."

Her face remained impassive but Jennifer detected a subtle shift in Rebecca's posture.

"I was looking through your eyes at the road where Summer was killed. Your phone had begun ringing and it had fallen onto the floor. You reached over to pick it up, taking your eyes off the road. You knew you had hit something because you heard the sound it made and felt the car's impact. When you stopped, you didn't bother getting out of the car because you couldn't see anything in the road, and you hadn't seen Summer before you leaned over so you didn't know she was there. That's why you drove off. But you must have known later that it was you. Why haven't you turned yourself in?"

"You can't possibly be serious. Do you really think I would have done something like that? Or that I would be doing all this..." she waved her hand at the room to indicate her involvement with the memorial, "if I had been the one who killed Summer?" she asked, her voice rising and her face turning red.

Jennifer remained calm.

"You can deny it all you want, but you and I both know it's true. You can't hide this forever, Becky. It will destroy you to try to live with this weighing on you. And Summer's parents deserve to know what happened. The memorial is a wonderful tribute, and you should be commended for all you've done to make it happen, but they need closure. Please think about making this right. I would understand if you don't want to turn yourself in before the event, but please do the right thing."

"I think you should leave now," Rebecca said, her voice icy.

CHAPTER TWENTY-NINE

Jennifer hesitated, searching Rebecca's face for any sign that her words had made an impact but all she saw was anger. She thought about adding more but changed her mind and left.

When she got to her car, she phoned Detective Roberts to let him know she had spoken to Rebecca.

"I told Rebecca about my vision but wasn't surprised when she denied everything. She looked rattled, though. She was angry, but the impression I got was it more about having been accused rather than me having known she was the one behind the wheel."

"That's fine. It's about what I expected. Detective Smith and I are following up with a body shop in Newport next week. It's a one-man operation and the owner was on his way out of town for a few days or we'd go sooner. "

"This might not be possible, but is there any chance that you could hold off on making an arrest until after the memorial service if you can prove it was Rebecca? I'm not suggesting you let her get away with it, of course, just delay an arrest. We're so close to the service and it would be too bad to have to cancel or postpone it because we weren't able to coordinate everything without her."

"I can't make any promises, but I understand your concern. If there's any way to do that, I'm sure we'll do our best."

"Thank you, Phil. I understand you have a job to do."

Jennifer had a feeling he would make good on his word. There was still time to convince Rebecca to turn herself in after the event, she reminded herself. The question was how could she do that?

CHAPTER THIRTY

Rebecca's hands shook so badly she had to clasp them together and take several deep breaths before she was able to compose herself and leave. She wanted to make sure she waited long enough for Jennifer to be gone. The last thing she needed was to run into her in the parking lot. She left by the back entrance, only partially opening the door so she could peek around it to check the cars still there without being seen. Relieved to find the only cars in the lot were hers and the weekend janitor's, she let the door close behind her and hurried to her car. As soon as she was safely inside, she used her mirrors to take one final look around before starting the engine and leaving the parking lot.

How could she possibly have known what happened? There was no one other than me there. And seriously? Psychometry? What kind of crap was that? Does she really expect me to believe her? She described exactly what happened inside my car, though. I'm going to have to be very careful around her.

Once home, she headed straight for the refrigerator where she had a bottle of wine chilling. She knew she shouldn't, but she could no longer make it through the day without dulling her senses with alcohol. *At least I'm waiting until I get home*, she rationalized. She made a promise to herself she wouldn't ever drink and drive again and, so far, she was mostly keeping that promise. She had slipped last Saturday but that had been the only time. A nightmare the night before had woken her gasping for air and drenched in sweat. She'd needed that drink to settle her nerves.

Reaching into her cupboard, she took out a water glass and filled it with the wine. She'd given up on wine glasses weeks ago. Gulping that one down to take the edge off, she then poured another to take with her to the living room and turned on the TV. It was set to her streaming service's channel. Despite having suggested to the committee to watch the interview on Channel 6, she wouldn't be. The local news channels were off limits even though none of them had been talking about updates of the accident since the week it happened.

She picked up her glass to take another drink and was surprised to see her glass was already empty. It was taking more alcohol to numb herself and after her run-in with Jennifer Ryder, she wasn't sure one bottle of wine would be enough tonight. An hour later, though, she had nodded off in her recliner and was dreaming.

It was the day of the accident, and she was seeing the stretch of road where the accident had happened. She could feel the cool air coming from the vents on the dashboard and there was music playing on the radio. Her phone rang and she reached over to pick it up from the floor. When she looked back up, she was horrified to see Summer Williams just as the car hit her. A voice was telling her *Just turn yourself in, Rebecca. Confess and take the consequences. This can all be over. You can't go on like this.*

She woke with a start with the glow of the television providing the only light in the room. Raising her hands to cover her face, she wept.

CHAPTER THIRTY-ONE

"Are you sure we're going the right way?" Phil Roberts asked Dennis Smith.

They had been traveling down a poorly maintained gravel road for the last five miles providing a bumpy ride and the distance between houses was growing longer adding to the concern that they were on the wrong route. It had taken several days of tracking down and making phone calls to independent body repair shops in a ten-mile radius of Bangor before connecting with A-One Auto Body Repair in Newport. They then had to wait another frustrating week to interview the owner in person but the information he'd given them over the phone had sounded promising.

"You can see the GPS as well as I can. If we're going the wrong way, it's because of that," Dennis replied testily. "Not to mention that you're the one who put in the address."

Phil gave him a look but kept quiet.

"Sorry. I didn't mean to snap at you," Dennis apologized.

"This case has been wearing on me. I just hope this trip pans out so we can wrap it up for the Williams family."

"I get it. I feel the same way," Phil said. "If this guy's records confirm what he told us on the phone, we should be able to at least bring Rebecca McCormick in for questioning."

"You and I both know it's circumstantial evidence. We can't tie her to the accident if she decides to lie about why she had her car repaired. We're going to have to get a confession."

"From what Jennifer Ryder told me, she's showing signs of breaking down. It might be just enough to put her over the edge if we can confront her with the repair invoices. She had to have thought she could keep it quiet by coming all the way out here and paying cash so it won't show up on her credit cards."

"Let's hope so," Phil replied. "After coming all this way, getting a confession would make it worth it."

Your destination is on the right in half a mile the GPS voice chirped.

"At least one thing is going right," Dennis said when they saw the sign for A-One Auto Body.

They turned into the driveway of a ranch house with a detached garage. It was a hot day for late September and the door of one of the bays was open providing a view of a man removing a dented fender from an SUV. He looked in their direction as they pulled up and parked their car. He wiped his hands on a rag that he produced from a pocket in his coveralls and walked out to greet them. He was in his fifties, tall and thin, with a ruddy complexion and receding hairline. What was left of it was a dark brown.

"Gary Newman?" Dennis asked when he got out of the car.

"That's me. You the detectives?"

"I'm Detective Smith and this is Detective Roberts," Dennis introduced them, and they each held up their badges.

"I keep all my paperwork inside. Follow me."

Gary led them into the house and a small neatly organized office which might have been a bedroom at one time.

"Lucky for you my wife takes care of all the bookkeeping. Otherwise, it would have taken me a week just to clean off my desk to find the invoices," he said, picking up a file that had been placed in the center of his desk and handing it over.

Phil took the file and examined the paperwork which included pictures of the damage to the car, an invoice for the parts ordered, the work order signed by Rebecca McCormick, and a copy of the receipt for payment which also had her signature as acknowledgement that the work had been completed to her satisfaction.

"Could you give us a copy of this?" he asked when he had finished looking through the file.

"Sure, no problem. I can do that right here on my printer."

After Gary had made the copies and handed them over, Dennis reached into his suit pocket and pulled out a six pack. Laying the photos on the desk, he asked "Can you tell us if one of these is the Rebecca McCormick whose car you repaired?"

Without hesitation he pointed to the photo of Rebecca taken from her driver's license.

"That's her. She claimed she'd hit a deer."

"Is there any chance you still have the damaged parts?" Dennis asked.

"As a matter of fact, I do. I can't explain it, but something felt off about her story. She seemed nervous and I got the impression she was hiding something, but I couldn't exactly call her a liar. I had this intuition that I should hang onto them, so instead of throwing them in the dumpster, I put them up on a shelf. Do you want them?"

"That would be very helpful, Mr. Newman. Would you be willing to submit to having a cheek swab taken to rule out your DNA?"

Suddenly it clicked with Phil where Dennis was going with this.

"No, I don't mind at all if it will help you catch the driver of the hit and run. It might not be this Rebecca McCormick, but if it is, I wouldn't want to be the one who helped her get away with it."

"Do you have a new trash bag that we could put the parts in?" Phil asked.

"Absolutely! I'll go get a few. It will probably take more than one."

"Let's get that cheek swab first. Would you get one of the kits, Dennis?"

A few minutes later, they had the cheek swab sample and Gary left to get the trash bags.

"That was brilliant, Dennis," Phil told him. "This could be just the break we need. If there's any DNA on the parts that matches Summer's, this could go from circumstantial to tangible evidence."

"Thanks! We should probably go with him to bag up the parts," Dennis said just seconds before Gary returned.

"We can put the parts in the bags if you can show us where they are," Phil said.

"No problem at all."

They followed Gary back to the garage and after they each donned a pair of latex gloves, Phil and Dennis put the headlight and fender into the trash bags and loaded them in the trunk of their car.

"We can't thank you enough, Mr. Newman," Dennis said and he and Phil both shook Gary's hand. They each handed him one of their business cards as well. "If you think of anything else, you can call either of us at the number on the card."

CHAPTER THIRTY-TWO

The detectives had let Jennifer know they had found the shop that had repaired Rebecca's car and had a stroke of luck that the parts were still there. They had put a rush on the request for testing for DNA, but the results had not arrived before the day of the memorial service. Rebecca had continued to treat Jennifer the same during their committee meetings, but it didn't escape her that she'd made a point of never being alone with her after Jennifer told her about her vision.

Early on the morning of the memorial service, the entire quilt club, including its part-time member, Sharon, had shown up to help Jennifer display the quilt donations. Paul was unable to help as it was a workday for him at Quilting Essentials, but his absence was more than made up for by those who had volunteered to help from the memorial committee. The response for donations from the community had been overwhelming; far exceeding Jennifer's expectations. The rental company insured by Jennifer and David had come through for them, donating the use of PVC racks for the displays. They set the racks up around the perimeter of the room, covered them with canvas drop cloths donated by a local hardware store, and attached the quilts to them with extra-large safety pins. Each quilt had the label Jennifer had supplied pinned to the front of it so that the name of the quilter could be seen by those attending the service. By the time they were done two hours later, the cafeteria had been transformed into an art installation of a rainbow of colors that evoked the very essence of summer.

"It's just beautiful," Jennifer said, her voice soft and tears welling in her eyes as she looked around the room.

"I couldn't agree more," Eva said, nodding her head.

"Summer's parents are going to be blown away," Sarah said.

"This is going to be a very special day for them and the entire community," Annalise offered her thoughts.

"The only thing that could make it better would be to have an arrest of the driver once it's over," Jennifer said.

"Have the detectives been in touch?" Sarah asked.

"Dennis called this morning to let me know they were very close to getting the DNA results. He told me that they may have found a thread in the headlight that matches the fiber of Summer's shorts, too. If they do, along with the DNA, he felt they won't have any problem getting an arrest warrant."

"Do you think Rebecca will confess?" Sarah asked.

Jennifer thought a moment. "She's been avoiding me ever since I told her I know she's the driver other than when it's absolutely necessary at the committee meetings. She's trying to hide it with more makeup than usual, but the shadows under her eyes are still obvious, and she has a haunted look about her. The guilt has to be having its effect. She has a lot to lose either way. Whether trying to hold onto her reputation at the expense of her mental and emotional well-being is worth it remains to be seen."

The members of the reception committee were filing in to set up the tables and chairs for the attendees following the memorial service. Jennifer realized that was the cue for the quilt club members to leave.

"Thanks again for all your help, ladies. I'm going to go home, get some rest, and finish polishing up my speech before I have to get ready for tonight. I'll see you back here in a few hours!"

CHAPTER THIRTY-THREE

The auditorium was filled to capacity with students, teachers, and members of the community. The room's atmosphere was a strange dichotomy of anticipation and solemnity. Many of Summer's classmates had clustered together in the seats near the front of the auditorium and as Jennifer's eyes panned over the serious young faces, she knew this was an event that would forever impact their lives. Everyone knew this was a celebration of life but one which should not have been taking place for someone who had been so full of life and whose life had been taken away much too soon. There was a cloth covered table on the stage of the auditorium with a poster-size picture of Summer on an easel and a bouquet of sunflowers, her favorite flower, beside it. A video montage of photos taken of her from her infancy to the time just before her death, as well as others taken with her classmates and the organizations she had volunteered with, was displayed on a screen at the back of the stage. A playlist of her favorite songs was playing in the background. The front row seats had been reserved for

Summer's family and members of the Memorial Service committee.

Jennifer, David, Matthew, and Nicole arrived together and made their way to the front of the auditorium where Jennifer left them to sit in her assigned seat after saying hello to the quilt club ladies. Eva and Jim Davis, Annalise, and Sarah and Ashley Pascal had saved seats for the Ryders in the second row. Sharon and Joseph Ramos had also joined them, filling up the seats in that section.

"Jennifer is looking especially pretty tonight," Eva told David who was sitting on her left.

"I couldn't agree more. She bought a new outfit just for the occasion and has been stressing over her speech about the blanket donations for the past week. I think she's rewritten it at least ten times. To say she's nervous would be an understatement," he replied with a smile.

"She's done a terrific job pulling it all together. Did you get a chance to peek in the cafeteria to see the display?"

"No, we got here too late. The parking lot was more crowded than we expected. I dropped the girls off at the front entrance so they wouldn't have as far to walk in heels but Matt and I had a hike once we found a parking spot. By then we didn't have enough time, but I can't wait to see it."

"It's amazing! All the quilters outdid themselves. The Bangor News came with a photographer and Channel 6 came, too, to cover the service. Jennifer told me she's taken a picture of every quilt and plans to put together an album along with a copy of the program for the Williams family as a keepsake," Eva said.

"That's right. She's been doing that as they've come in so it shouldn't take her too long to put that together. I know she's doing this from her heart and I'm glad she is, but it will be good for her to rest once it's done. I don't think she realizes how much energy she's put into it."

"We've told her we'll help with the thank you notes so she

doesn't have to take that on all by herself. We'll make sure that happens," Eva reassured him.

Their attention was drawn to the stage where Rebecca McCormick was walking to the podium and the music that had been playing stopped alerting the crowd that the service was about to begin.

"Thank you all for coming tonight for this celebration of Summer Williams." Her voice caught and she cleared her throat before continuing. "There will be a reception in the cafeteria immediately following the memorial service. As you can see from the program, we have several speakers tonight beginning with Principal Jackson." She nodded to him, and he climbed the stairs to the stage and the podium as Rebecca retreated behind the curtain to his right. He was followed by several teachers and students who had volunteered to eulogize Summer. There were moments of laughter as stories were told of Summer's vivacious personality and moments of sadness when they spoke of how much they would miss her. Many in the audience were wiping tears from the corners of their eyes and the sound of people blowing their noses could be heard throughout the auditorium. When the last of them had taken their turn, Rebecca returned to the podium.

"I'd like to ask for a round of applause for our next speaker, Jennifer Ryder. If you haven't already seen the exhibit of quilts hanging in the cafeteria, I hope you'll stop before you leave tonight. She was the organizer for this project and is going to tell us about its significance. Jennifer ..."

Jennifer climbed the stairs to the stage. She had typed her speech on her tablet which she placed on the podium and took a deep breath before beginning.

"Summer Williams was a blessing. My children, Matthew and Nicole, who are here tonight, grew up with Summer and attended elementary school and high school with her. She would have graduated with Matthew this year. They had many conversations at our house discussing which colleges they would apply to and critiquing each other's submission essay. My daughter, Nicole, was on the track team with Summer and they often ran together to keep up with their training for the team. Our community of Glen Lake has lost a valuable volunteer and team leader for its community recreation department programs.

'When I first learned of Summer's death, I knew I wanted to do something special to celebrate her life and spoke to my quilting club, The Cozy Quilts Club, about it. Knowing how much Summer loved children and her plans to become a teacher, we thought what better way to honor her memory than by making quilts to donate to Project Linus. For those of you who don't know about Project Linus, their primary purpose is to provide blankets in the US to children ranging in age from infancy to eighteen who are seriously ill, traumatized, or otherwise in need. The blankets must be new, handmade, and washable. We've provided a link to their website on tonight's program for anyone who would like to learn more about this organization.

'My fellow founding quilt club members, Eva Perkins, Annalise Jordan, and Sarah Pascal, are here tonight along with our honorary members, Sharon Ramos and Paul Taylor, and I'd like to acknowledge them for all the work they've done to make this project a success because I couldn't have done it without them."

Jennifer paused as the audience spontaneously started applauding.

"That wasn't the end of it, though. Even as much as we love quilting, there's no way our quilt club could have made all of the ones hanging in the cafeteria tonight. I told the Memorial Committee about our idea and asked if anyone would like to join us and from there the project snowballed. I didn't anticipate the response we received and the generosity of our community, but I should have. We now have over fifty quilts. Would everyone who donated a blanket please stand so we can give you a round of applause?"

The donors stood, many looking self-conscious, as handclapping filled the auditorium and then was followed by a standing ovation.

"We hope this gesture will bring comfort not only to the children who will be receiving the blankets, but to the Williams family as well, to know how much we loved Summer," Jennifer continued once the clapping faded out and everyone had resumed their seats.

She looked down at the Williams to see Roger with his arm around Debbie. They both nodded their acknowledgement to Jennifer, and she saw the tears misting in their eyes. As she was picking up her tablet to leave the stage, she saw Detectives Smith and Roberts standing at the back of the auditorium. They gave her a nod and she realized they were there to arrest Rebecca. True to their word, they had waited for the end of the memorial. Jennifer turned to Rebecca who was approaching the podium from where she'd been standing in the wing and their eyes met. Jennifer's back was to the audience as she quietly told her, "Do the right thing," and then walked back to her seat.

Rattled by her words, Rebecca walked to the podium and gripped the sides to steady herself. She began to speak but the words stuck in her throat. She cleared her throat and tried again.

"This is the conclusion of this portion of our celebration and as I'd mentioned earlier, there are refreshments in the caf..." She couldn't speak as the sobs she'd been choking down began despite her efforts to suppress them. Her hands clenched the podium even tighter as she felt her knees shaking.

"I just can't do this anymore. I can't go on living this lie."

Tears streamed down her face.

The room had become completely silent as everyone stared in shock.

"I didn't know. I didn't know," she repeated, looking

beseechingly at the Williams and her voice pleading. "Please forgive me. I didn't mean to hit her. I didn't see her..." She collapsed to her knees and put her hands over her face, but they couldn't keep the wails from escaping her body.

By this time the detectives had reached the stage and walked up the stairs to Rebecca. They each held her arm on either side to help her stand and walked with her to the wings and the back of the stage.

The crowd erupted into a cacophony of conversations all asking the same question—*what just happened?*

CHAPTER THIRTY-FOUR

Principal Jackson bolted from his seat and returned to the stage, trying to bring order to the chaos.

"Ladies and gentlemen, you're welcome to make your way to the cafeteria for the reception and the quilt exhibit. Thank you all for coming this evening to honor Summer," and turning his back to the crowd, he walked briskly to the back of the stage where the detectives were waiting.

"What is going on?" he asked them.

"We've just placed Ms. McCormick under arrest for vehicular manslaughter in the death of Summer Williams. She's been read her her rights. Is there another way to exit the building without going back through the auditorium?" Dennis Smith asked.

Principal Jackson looked from them to Rebecca, his eyes wide and his mouth slightly agape as he processed what he'd been told. Recovering his composure, he pointed toward the left.

"Yes, there's a stage door we can use. Follow me."

A patrol car had accompanied the detectives to the high

school but was parked at the front of the building. They radioed in instructions to meet them at the stage door and after Rebecca was placed inside, it left to take her to the police station. Smith and Roberts followed Principal Jackson back to the auditorium. While he hurried the last of the stragglers out of the auditorium and closed the doors to give them privacy, the detectives made their way to the Williams who were still sitting, too stunned to move, but rose when they saw them approaching.

"Mr. and Mrs. Williams, we've just arrested Rebecca McCormick and charged her with vehicular manslaughter in the death of your daughter," Phil Roberts told them after they had introduced themselves.

"Rebecca McCormick?" Debbie said in disbelief despite what they had just witnessed. "That has to be a mistake."

She turned to Roger as if expecting him to tell her they were wrong. His face was set and his eyes were hard.

"You have proof?" he asked them.

"Yes. We found the body shop where she had her car repaired. We got lucky and the owner had kept the parts, so we were able to send them to the state crime lab to be analyzed. They found DNA and fibers from the clothing Summer was wearing that day. She as much as confessed just now but once she has a lawyer, she could still enter a not guilty plea. I can't make any promises, of course, but I don't think a jury would acquit her based on the evidence we have and about 200 witnesses to her confession," Phil said.

"We apologize for not speaking with you earlier, but the results didn't arrive until this morning, and we had to do the paperwork to get an arrest warrant. It didn't all come together until the memorial had already begun," Dennis added.

Debbie turned to Roger and buried her head on his chest. He wrapped his arms around her shoulders to comfort her as sobs shook her body.

"Thank you," he told the detectives as one tear escaped and

ran down his left cheek. Leaning down, he kissed the top of Debbie's head and turned to his right where their daughter, Emma, was still sitting and reached out to wrap her hand in his and squeezed.

"We'll be in touch, but we should get to the station so we can question Ms. McCormick," Phil Roberts said.

Jennifer had hung back after the other ladies in the quilt club offered to step in for her at the reception until she could join them. David, Matt, and Nicole left to attend the reception as well knowing she wanted to speak with the detectives and the Williams family. Phil and Dennis saw her waiting and walked over to her.

"I'd like to think we would have reached the same result with this case, but we got there a lot quicker with your help," Dennis said.

"Dennis is right. Thank you," Phil agreed.

"It was a team effort," Jennifer told them. "I think I can speak for all the ladies in the quilt club to say we'd be glad to offer our help if you ever need it again."

"We may just take you up on that," Phil said, a grin tugging at the corners of his mouth.

"I look forward to seeing you again," Dennis said, and they turned to walk out.

She went to where the Williams and Principal Jackson were standing. Jennifer reached out to Debbie and gave her a hug.

"This has been an emotional day. I don't think anyone would blame you if you left without attending the reception. Principal Jackson, is there a way for them to leave without having to go through the foyer?"

"Of course, we can use the stage entrance where they took Rebecca out."

Debbie looked at Roger and Emma before replying to Jennifer. "Unless you would like to stay, I think I'd like to go home. I don't think I can face anyone or answer any questions."

"That's fine with me," Roger said, and Emma nodded her agreement.

"If there's anything I can do, let me know," Jennifer said.

"I will," Debbie said, reaching out to touch Jennifer's arm before turning to join Roger and Emma as Principal Jackson led them out the back entrance.

CHAPTER THIRTY-FIVE

*J*ennifer returned to the cafeteria and found the others sitting together at a table near the back of the room. Judging by the size of the crowd, she guessed at least half of all those attending the memorial service were still here. Several people eyed her curiously, perhaps hoping to receive some news about what they had just witnessed but were disappointed when they realized none was forthcoming.

"How is it going here?" she asked.

"After what just happened, I'm surprised anyone can focus on the quilts, but they seem to be a nice distraction," Eva said.

Jennifer could hear appreciative oohs and ahhs as throngs of people made their way around the room admiring the quilts and the refreshments were a hit, too, judging by the line waiting for their turn to fill their plates and cups.

"What happened after we left?" David asked.

"Phil and Dennis came back to let the Williams know they arrested Rebecca and she'd been taken to the police station for booking and then Principal Jackson took them out the back way so they wouldn't have to go through the crowd on their way out."

"That's good. They have enough to deal with right now," Annalise said.

"They do, but maybe now that they have some closure, they can begin to heal," Sarah offered.

They all nodded their agreement and were silent for a moment.

"Well, unless you need us for anything, I'm going to find Matt and Nicole and head home," David broke the silence.

Jennifer had already arranged to ride home with Annalise after the reception was over. All the quilt club members had offered to help take down the quilts and split them up between them to stitch the labels on the back before donating them.

"We'll be fine. I'll see you in a couple hours."

The crowd was finally thinning forty-five minutes later with only five minutes left before the official end time. Jennifer looked around the cafeteria and noticed Sandy Greene from the Reception Committee with a trash bag in hand clearing the empty tables of any cups and plates left behind.

"I should probably check with the other committee members to make sure we're all set to wrap this up. There wasn't much that Rebecca would have had to do now but without her here they may be wondering. It's probably fine to start taking the quilts down now. I don't see anyone waiting to see them."

"That works for me," Jim said as he stood and held his hand out to Eva to help her up. The others followed his cue.

"Sarah and I will get the boxes to pack them in. They should still be in the corner behind the display racks," Annalise said.

Jennifer had to admit that Rebecca had done an excellent job organizing the event. Everyone she spoke with understood what their tasks were and could carry on without her presence, and Principal Jackson stepped in to make sure the school would be closed up properly. The quilts removed and boxed, everyone walked to their respective cars with Jennifer joining Annalise and said their goodbyes.

CHAPTER THIRTY-SIX

Two weeks later, the Williams family was hosting a gathering to thank the Memorial Service organizers. The Cozy Quilts Club including Sharon and Paul, were in attendance along with all the other committee members with one obvious exception. Rebecca had been released on bail and pleaded not guilty at her arraignment as Phil Roberts had predicted. It was a much more joyous occasion this time and Jennifer detected a change in Debbie and Roger's demeanor. There was still sadness but the strained look around their eyes she had observed when she had seen them before the memorial was gone and they looked rested. Even Emma was in better spirits. Nicole had come with Jennifer to keep Emma company while the adults mingled and when Jennifer looked over to the corner where they were sitting, both girls were animatedly talking and laughing. It warmed Jennifer's heart to see them.

"It's like a weight has been lifted from all of us and I have my little girl back. I was worried about her, but I think she's going to be okay," Debbie said.

Jennifer hadn't been aware that Debbie had joined her, she was so absorbed in watching the girls.

"I think you're all going to be okay. I haven't seen you looking so relaxed and happy since before the accident."

"According to Detective Roberts, you're partially responsible for Rebecca's arrest."

"Did he say why he thought that?" Jennifer asked, butterflies fluttering in her stomach.

"He said you gave them a tip that helped lead them in her direction and without it, they might not have been able to learn the identity of the driver. He didn't say what that was, but it would be up to you whether you wanted to tell me."

Jennifer could see that Debbie wanted to know but would she believe it if she told her the truth? And would she keep Jennifer's secret? She didn't think she was ready for it to become public knowledge that she had the ability of psychometry.

"He's giving me too much credit. I noticed some changes in Rebecca while we were working together on the committee, and I realized she drove a silver four door sedan that looked like it might recently have been repaired. It occurred to me her behavior might be caused by guilt if it was her. I mentioned it to them, but they took it from there. The credit should go to them for following up and not dismissing what I told them, especially since it was a bit of a stretch to think it could be her." Jennifer hoped her white lie was convincing Debbie.

"Thank you for taking the risk. A lot of people wouldn't have."

Jennifer hadn't realized she was holding her breath but let it out as naturally as she could. She gave Debbie a hug both as comfort and a way to hide the relief that was probably showing on her face.

"I should make my rounds with the others, but I wanted to make sure I had a chance to speak with you about the tip when no one else was listening and this seemed like the perfect time."

"Of course. Maybe we can get together for coffee or lunch soon?"

"I'd love that," Debbie told her and went to join some of the other guests.

Annalise had walked over to Jennifer and gave her a grin.

"You look like the cat who swallowed the canary."

"You could say that," Jennifer agreed with a smile. "Phil Roberts told Debbie I had given them a tip that led to Rebecca's arrest."

Annalise's eyebrows rose.

"He didn't tell her how I got that information but told her it was up to me whether I wanted to share it. I decided it would be better to tell a white lie. I'm not ready to go public yet."

"I understand. It's not something I share unless I know I can trust that person to understand it's information for their ears only. I'm not sure we're going to be able to keep our abilities secret much longer, though, if we keep getting drawn into solving murders."

"With any luck, there won't be more of them," Jennifer said.

"Don't count on it," Annalise said giving her a wink and walking off to find Eva and Sarah.

Jennifer looked around to locate David, needing his stability. Annalise's words had unnerved her, and she realized it was because she suspected she was right. Glen Lake was a small town and secrets were hard to keep. She would need to have a long talk with David later and get his advice. It wouldn't be just her who would be affected. She had to consider how people would react not just to her but to her entire family, but for now, it was time to enjoy the party. She took the opportunity to slip out to her car to retrieve the scrapbook she had made with pictures of all the quilts that had been donated and in some cases the quilter had written a personal message of their memories of Summer and best wishes for the Williams. She gathered the quilt club to be with her before tapping a glass to catch everyone's attention. The room quieted and all eyes were on Jennifer.

"Debbie, Roger, Emma, you didn't get the chance to look at all the quilts hanging in the auditorium on the night of Summer's memorial service. I intended to do this anyway and I'm so glad I did because now I can present you with this album with a picture of every single one. Many of the quilters have included messages as well and each and every one of us hope that this gesture will bring you happiness when you look at it. Summer was so very special to us, and we will miss her. I think she would be pleased knowing that so many children will be touched both physically and emotionally by these gifts in her honor."

She handed the album to Debbie who clutched it to her chest before giving Jennifer a hug and whispering *thank you* in her ear. Many of the guests were wiping their eyes and only an enormous amount of self-control was keeping Jennifer from crying now, too.

"We will treasure this always. You mentioned that you would be sending out thank you notes to all the quilters. Do you think it would be okay if I added a message as well?" Debbie asked.

"Of course. What a wonderful gesture! I know everyone will be thrilled by it."

Roger cleared his throat. "I'd like to raise a toast." As everyone found their glass and raised it, he said simply "To Summer and the people who loved her." That was all that was needed.

CHAPTER THIRTY-SEVEN

∽

A week had passed since Rebecca's arrest and arraignment. The trial date wouldn't be for several months, but she had resigned from her position at the high school, and no one had heard from her. That didn't surprise Jennifer. Under the circumstances, she would have been more surprised if Rebecca had continued teaching, assuming the school board allowed her to do so.

Jennifer was concentrating on her sewing at the regular Cozy Quilts Club meeting thinking about Rebecca's situation when she felt a hand on her shoulder. Startled out of her reverie, she dropped the pieces she had been aligning prior to stitching them together. She looked up to find Annalise beside her.

"You should call her." Her voice was low so that only Jennifer could hear. When Jennifer's eyebrows raised, Annalise continued. "You were thinking about Rebecca, and you're worried about her."

Jennifer didn't need to ask how Annalise knew what she was thinking.

"I'm afraid she won't take my call. She's probably angry thinking I'm the one who got her arrested."

"She might," Annalise agreed. "But try anyway. She needs someone right now."

Jennifer nodded. "You're right. I can at least try."

Annalise patted her shoulder once again and returned to her sewing station. By the end of the evening, Jennifer had come up with a plan.

CHAPTER THIRTY-EIGHT

~

Rebecca hadn't stepped outside her door since she returned home after the humiliation of being arrested a week ago. She had plenty of food and her appetite was practically nonexistent, so going to the grocery store hadn't been an issue. She'd lost ten pounds before her arrest and another five pounds since but, for once, wasn't happy the scales were on a downward trajectory. Taking the coward's way out, she had emailed Principal Jackson with her resignation. There was no way she could face anyone after what she'd done.

Did I take a shower yesterday? She gazed at her reflection in the bathroom mirror, hardly recognizing the woman with greasy hair and red-rimmed eyes staring back at her. For a brief moment she thought she could muster the energy to turn on the shower but reconsidered and shuffled back out of the bathroom in the same sweats she'd worn the day before. *Why bother? What's the point?* As she passed by the front door on her way to the living room, she noticed the pile of mail on the floor that had been deposited through the mail chute. Sighing, she changed directions and shambled over to pick it up and shuffled through the envelopes. Most were offers from credit card companies that would end up in the bin of her shredder, but an envelope addressed to her that had been handwritten with a return address for Jennifer Ryder made her pause in mid-shuffle. She stood staring at the envelope as though transfixed. Her hands were shaking slightly as she turned it over to open the seal with her finger.

> Dear Rebecca,
>
> I can only imagine how you must be feeling. I've been worried about you and even though I'm probably the last person you want to hear from, I wanted to take the chance.
>
> I saw what happened that day through your eyes and in that moment, I knew you didn't realize you had hit Summer, or you never would have left the scene. I want you to know that I believe you. I also felt the conflict you were going through and the guilt you had about not turning yourself in right away. The only reason I can think of why you didn't, was that you were scared about what the consequences would be. There was a lot on the line for you.
>
> Others may not agree, but I also want you to know that I believe your motives for heading up the memorial committee were pure and what you did to put together the service came from your heart and a genuine desire to honor Summer's memory.

You may be thinking that no one wants to have anything to do with you, but that's not true. You can always reach out to me.
Jennifer

Rebecca balled the letter up in her fist as at first a wave of anger filled her, but it was immediately replaced with wails pouring out from what felt like the very depths of her soul and her knees buckled. She remained on her knees on the floor, her head bowed and the letter still in her fist clutched to her chest until at last, her sobs subsided. Her shoulders slumped with exhaustion. Taking a deep breath, she unfolded the letter and read through it again. And again. Rising to stand, she placed it on the table beside her favorite living room chair and walked back to the bathroom to shower.

CHAPTER THIRTY-NINE

"Jennifer?"

If she hadn't seen Rebecca's name on the screen, Jennifer would never have recognized the tentative voice speaking her name.

"Rebecca. I'm so glad you called. I wasn't sure that you would."

"I wasn't sure that I would either. I want to thank you for your letter. I've lost count of how many times I've read it."

"I hope it helped."

"It did. More than you know. I still can't face anyone, but I'm taking better care of myself now."

"That's important."

"It gave me the strength to make the decision to do what's right. I called my lawyer and told her I'm going to plead guilty. You were right that I didn't realize I'd hit Summer but as soon as I did, I should have turned myself in. I was worried about what would happen to me if I did, but the police found out anyway and it only made things worse. It won't bring Summer back, but

I want to pay my debt and if that means going to jail, then so be it."

"I don't know what to say, Rebecca... Jennifer paused, gathering her thoughts. "You're doing the right thing. It was a tragic accident, but I hope someday you'll be able to forgive yourself."

"Right now, I don't see that happening."

There was a pause before Rebecca spoke again.

"I have a favor to ask you."

"Okay."

"Do you think the Williams would agree to talk to me? I want to apologize to them."

Jennifer had not been expecting that.

"I honestly don't know, Rebecca. Would you like me to ask on your behalf?"

Jennifer heard Rebecca let out her breath.

"I would be so grateful if you would. And I know I'm asking a lot, but would you be with me if they agree to see me?"

"Does your attorney know about this?" she asked, avoiding the question.

"She didn't think I should but since there won't be a trial now, it wouldn't affect my case, so she left it up to me."

Jennifer didn't answer immediately. She realized, though, that it would be best for everyone if there was a neutral party present.

"I can't make any promises, but I'll see what I can do and let you know."

CHAPTER FORTY

Jennifer's stomach was tied in knots as she waited for someone at the Williams home to answer her call. She heard Debbie's voice saying hello and willed herself to break through her nervousness to deliver Rebecca's request. She had discussed it with David the night before. At first he tried to dissuade her from getting in the middle but as she explained that her intuition was telling her it could be a positive step for everyone to move forward, he relented.

"I'm not a hundred percent on board with this but you make a good point. I just hope you don't get caught in the crossfire if it doesn't go well. Do you want me to be with you?"

"A part of me says yes, but maybe it's better if you don't. Rebecca might feel like she's being ganged up on if there are too many people involved."

"Debbie. It's Jennifer Ryder."

"Jennifer. It's so good to hear from you."

"I hope you still think so after I explain why I'm calling." She paused to gather her courage and pressed on. "I received a call from Rebecca McCormick. She asked if I would reach out to you to arrange a meeting so she can apologize to all of you."

"She *what?*"

The words exploded through the telephone line and Jennifer was afraid she'd made a terrible misjudgment about how this would go.

"I can't believe she has the gall to even suggest it after what she did. You can tell her in no uncertain terms that we have no desire to see her."

This was not going well but Jennifer's gut was telling her to keep trying.

"I don't know if you've heard, but she told me she's going to plead guilty so there won't be a trial. This is against her lawyer's advice, but Rebecca knows it's what she should do. She can't change what happened but she's ready to accept the consequences. Apologizing to you is the other piece of making her amends but she understands you may not be ready for that. She asked if I would act as the go-between and be there if you agree to a meeting."

There was silence on the line and Jennifer checked the screen to see if the call had dropped.

"I didn't know, Jennifer. I'm glad to hear she's accepting responsibility, but it may be too much or too soon for us to face her. I'll talk to Roger and Emma and let you know."

"That's all I can ask."

CHAPTER FORTY-ONE

Scoops of chocolate cookie dough were lined up like soldiers on the cookie sheet and she was filling up a second sheet when Jennifer's phone rang. She'd almost given up hope that Debbie would call so was surprised to see she was the one on the line. Keeping her tone neutral she answered the phone.

"Jennifer, it's Debbie Williams. We've had some time to think about Rebecca's request and have had several discussions as a family. Roger and Nicole aren't ready for this. I didn't think I would be either, but after a lot of soul searching, I've decided I am. Would you still be there?"

"If that's what you want, I can do that."

They agreed to set up the meeting at Jennifer's house so it would be in neutral territory.

Jennifer scrolled through her Contacts for Rebecca's number and pressed the call button and waited through three rings before she answered.

"I almost didn't answer the phone because I was afraid of

what you would have to say. Did the Williams agree to meet me?"

"Only Debbie will. We've decided meeting at my house would be best. Can you be here on Tuesday at two?"

"I'll have to find a ride; my license has been suspended." Jennifer heard the embarrassment in Rebecca's voice.

"Oh, of course. I should have known that. Give me your address and I'll come to get you."

IF THEY HADN'T KNOWN it was Rebecca, neither Jennifer nor Debbie would have recognized the woman sitting at Jennifer's dining room table. Her clothes hung off her now frail body looking at least two sizes too big. Her face was gaunt and the makeup she'd applied did nothing to hide the dark purple shadows under her eyes. Her hands gave away her nervousness as her knuckles turned white from clasping them so tightly.

Jennifer ushered Debbie to the table and motioned for her to take a seat opposite Rebecca. The palpable tension in the room made it feel as though there was a weighted blanket covering them.

"Rebecca, would you like to begin?" Jennifer asked hoping to get this over with as soon as possible.

She nodded and Jennifer could see her swallow before beginning.

"I wouldn't blame you if you hate me, Debbie. I'm doing a good job of hating myself, too. There is nothing I wouldn't do if I could go back to that day and change what happened. I knew I shouldn't have taken my eyes off the road, but I thought I could… It doesn't matter and I don't want to make excuses for what I did. Period. I don't expect you to forgive me, but I want you to know how very, very sorry I am."

Debbie remained quiet, her eyes never leaving Rebecca's face.

"You destroyed our family, and you took a beautiful soul away from this world. There is no way that you can ever make up for that no matter how much time you'll spend in jail," she said, a hard edge in her voice. "I'm not ready to forgive you. Maybe someday, but not yet. I had to be sure that you really are sorry, and I needed to see your face and hear the words. I believe you."

Tears were streaming down Rebecca's cheeks. It was the response she'd expected but the words still stung. She knew she didn't deserve her forgiveness.

Debbie rose from her seat and walked around the table. Jennifer held her breath, not knowing whether she should prepare herself to come to Rebecca's defense if things turned physical. Rebecca drew back and it occurred to Jennifer that she might be thinking the same. Debbie's touch was gentle, though, as she took Rebecca's hand in hers.

"I meant what I said about not forgiving you now," Debbie said, her voice gentler now. "It's not healthy to carry this pain and anger with me forever, though. I know that. So I'm going to try to forgive you, but it will take time. I suspect a lot of time."

Rebecca's shoulders shook and the tears continued to roll down her cheeks and drip onto her blouse.

"Thank you," she said as she heaved in deep breaths. "That's all I can ask."

Debbie squeezed her hand and let it go.

"I need to go now but thank you for arranging this, Jennifer."

"I'll walk you out." Jennifer rose from her seat.

"There's no need. I can see myself out."

EPILOGUE

The Cozy Quilts Club was gathered at their regular meeting surrounded by quilts. The labels were sewn in; the last step and they were now ready to be donated. It was only the four of them at this meeting. Sharon had volunteered to babysit for her new grandchild so the parents could have a date night. Paul had a backlog of sewing machines that needed repairs and wanted to use the quiet time of working when the store was closed to catch up.

"It makes my heart sing every time I look at these beautiful quilts," Eva said as they were folding them to be put in the boxes that would be taken to Quilting Essentials.

"You can almost feel the love that was put into making them coming through," Annalise said.

"I stopped at the spot where Summer died a couple days ago but I didn't sense her presence. I think she knew it would be okay to move on now that her family is more at peace and Rebecca is being held responsible for her death," Sarah told them.

"Oh, I hope so," Jennifer said. She had filled them all in on the meeting between Rebecca and Debbie.

"I feel a little guilty that I wasn't able to come up with a way to let her family know she loves them."

"It's okay, Sarah. They know," Jennifer said.

"Sarah, my intuition has been sending me signals all night long. Is something upsetting you?" Annalise asked.

"Nothing gets by you, does it?" Sarah asked, teasing. "I hadn't planned to bring it up until I knew more. Earlier today I got a phone call from a friend of mine. She asked if she could stay with me and Ashley because the police wouldn't let her back into her apartment. She'd come back from a walk and found her roommate dead in their kitchen. She wanted to know if I could help. I don't have many of the details yet, but I think we may have another murder to solve," Sarah announced.

The others looked from one to another and slowly they each began to smile.

"We can't wait."

AFTERWORD

Project Linus is a real organization that has been donating blankets to needy children since 1995. With chapters in all 50 states, there may be a local chapter in your area. You can find out more about Project Linus at its website.

https://www.projectlinus.org/

ALSO BY MARSHA DEFILIPPO

Arizona Dreams

Deja vu Dreams

Disillusioned Dreams

A Cozy Quilts Club Mystery series

Follow the Crumbs

Finding the Treasure

Caught in a Spider's Web

Counting Coins

Pulling Out the Hidden Stitches

(Download the story by typing https://dl.bookfunnel.com/15vlqk2g9h in your choice of a browser window or use the QR code below.)

ABOUT THE AUTHOR

After retiring from her day job of nearly 33 years, Marsha DeFilippo has embarked on a new career of writing books. She is also a quilter and lifelong avid crafter who has yet to try a craft she doesn't like. She spends her winters in Arizona and the remainder of the year in Maine.

For more information, please visit my website:
marsha defilippo.com

To get the latest information on new releases, excerpts and more, be sure to sign up for Marsha's newsletter.
https://marshadefilippo.com/newsletter

facebook.com/Marsha-DeFilippo
instagram.com/marshadefilippo
amazon.com/author/marshadefilippo
bookbub.com/authors/marsha-defilippo
pinterest.com/defilippo0699

www.ingramcontent.com/pod-product-compliance
Lightning Source LLC
LaVergne TN
LVHW041040130325
805891LV00021B/103